KU-094-092

It was going to be a hair-splitter, for damn sure.

Bolan stepped into the open and cut sand at their feet with a burst from the chattergun.

Smiley Dublin took a dive to the side, yelling something at the hula girls as she did so. The Chinese whirled into the confrontation, the realisation of doom pulling at those not-so-inscrutable features. A bawling and milling erupted from the water's edge, with a brandishing of arms and a confusion of alarmed commands.

Bolan gave them to the first swell before fingering the little gadget at his belt. The two explosions came as one just as the canoes lifted into the swell. Bolan saw the twin flash and glimpsed hurtling fragments before the outriggers disappeared beyond the wall of water.

also by Don Pendleton

THE EXECUTIONER: MIAMI MASSACRE
THE EXECUTIONER: ASSAULT ON SOHO
THE EXECUTIONER: CHICAGO WIPEOUT
THE EXECUTIONER: VEGAS VENDETTA
THE EXECUTIONER: CARIBBEAN KILL
THE EXECUTIONER: CALIFORNIA HIT
THE EXECUTIONER: BOSTON BLITZ
THE EXECUTIONER: WASHINGTON I.O.U.
THE EXECUTIONER: SAN DIEGO SIEGE
THE EXECUTIONER: PANIC IN PHILLY
THE EXECUTIONER: NIGHTMARE IN NEW YORK
THE EXECUTIONER: JERSEY GUNS
THE EXECUTIONER: TEXAS STORM
THE EXECUTIONER: DETROIT DEATHWATCH
THE EXECUTIONER: FIREBASE SEATTLE
THE EXECUTIONER: NEW ORLEANS KNOCKOUT

and published by Corgi Books

Don Pendleton

Executioner 22:
HAWAIIAN HELLGROUND

CORGI BOOKS
A DIVISION OF TRANSWORLD PUBLISHERS LTD

EXECUTIONER 22:
HAWAIIAN HELLGROUND
A CORGI BOOK 0 552 10302 0

First publication in Great Britain

PRINTING HISTORY
Corgi edition published 1976

Copyright © 1975 by Pinnacle Books Inc.

Corgi Books are published by Transworld Publishers Ltd.,
Century House, 61–63 Uxbridge Road,
Ealing, London, W.5.
Made and printed in Great Britain by
Hunt Barnard Printing Ltd., Aylesbury, Bucks.

This is a work of fiction. All the characters and
events portrayed in this book are fictional, and
any resemblance to real people or incidents is
purely coincidental.

As MB would wish,
this book is dedicated
to those at *Puowaina*.
Live on!

dp

If I cannot bend Heaven,
I shall move Hell.

—Virgil

I would not attempt
to command Heaven—
but Hell I'll commandeer!

—Mack Bolan

Prologue

A tall, unmoving silhouette in black stood at the upper rim of the ancient crater known as the Punchbowl—officially, the National Memorial Cemetery of the Pacific, the battle monument to the nation's war dead. The Hawaiian word is Puowaina, translating literally as "Hill of Sacrifice."

Mack Bolan knew a thing or two about sacrifice in warfare.

Row upon row of stark white crosses marked the end of the trail for many other warriors who had made the ultimate sacrifice.

Bolan's brothers lay there—thousands of them.

He felt the movement of that place, identified with it, shivering lightly under the gently sighing wind that swept his face with the ghostly "hello" from thousands of dead young men.

"Live on," he replied quietly, and turned his gaze briefly to the light show below and afar—Pearl Harbor, Honolulu, Waikiki, finally Diamond Head looming as the natural horizon southward.

Paradise, sure—for some.

But not for Mack Bolan.

All of Bolan's trails led to hell, with no detours through paradise. That was hellground down there, and that was all it could be. The enemy was there.

Like ants at a picnic, they swarmed upon everything that was sacred, noble, or even good in the human experience—and there was much good to be looted from this youngest state of the union, this experiment in paradisical living.

Bolan had met them, this enemy, in many other places. This was to be the 22nd major campaign of the war. He'd never expected to live through the first. The combat trail had led him to many cities, many regions—but somehow he'd never expected it to bring him here, to this garden island. It had. And he was here, simply because the enemy was here—in massive force.

He'd come to the Punchbowl simply to commune awhile with his dead brothers, to say "hello" and "goodbye"—and perhaps to remind himself that Mack Bolan also lay there, in effect if not in fact.

All that had held meaning to the life of Mack Bolan had indeed ceased to exist many hard battles ago— all that was left was the mission itself and the hardcase warrior whom the entire world had come to know as the Executioner.

He lived only to kill.

Yeah. And what a hell of an excuse for life. Several times he had been tempted to check it in, to let it go, to resign the mission and life itself. It could be so easy . . . so damn easy. Every cop in the Western world wanted his hide. The entire world of organized crime wanted his head—the bounties for which had now pyramided to a half-million bloody bucks. Sure, it would be easy. Just let go. Just relax the vigil, for so much as a heartbeat—and, yeah, that heart would never beat again.

But it was also hard for Mack Bolan to die. There was a job to be done. He was probably the only man

2

living who had even an outside chance to do that job. So, sure . . . it was harder to die than to live.

So whoever said that life was just for laughs?

Life was for living, and a guy lived the hand that was dealt him. Those men beneath those crosses down there—they'd lived their hand to the bitter end.

Mack Bolan could do no less.

"I consecrate you," he quietly told them, then the Executioner went down to meet the enemy.

1: Aloha

Every war has to begin somewhere. For the Hawaiian mob, it began at the plush apartment of Paul Angliano, the drug trade's chief distributor for the Waikiki district. It had been a lucrative territory, with daily receipts averaging in the fifty-thousand-dollar range. Even so, it was a small beginning for a raging war which would rock that entire island state.

The Mafia boss of Waikiki was standing beside an open wall safe when the door exploded inward and black death strode into that room. Angliano had perhaps a single heartbeat to see what had come for him —and the final image recorded upon those doomed eyes could have been no more than a duplication of the same death image which had overhung and haunted the Mafia world from the beginning of Mack Bolan's personal war: a tall figure clad in black, a face chiseled from ice, a black pistol extended and silently chugging a pencil of flame—then a nasty red fountain erupted from between those shocked eyes and Paul John Angliano sloppily departed the world of men.

A military medal clattered to the desk as the only other occupant of the room—one Joey Puli, a Polynesian—staggered clear of the falling body and raised both hands in a desperate stretch for survival.

"Wait, *wait!*" Puli yelped, his horrified gaze bouncing from the remains of Angliano to another crumpled form which lay beyond the shattered doorway.

"I'll need a reason to wait," the voice of death responded.

"Hell, I—I don't even know the man!"

"Not good enough, Joey." The Beretta coughed again, sending a quiet whistler zipping into the floor between the guy's feet.

"Okay, okay!" Puli yelled, dancing backwards and coming to rest with his shoulders pressed to the wall. The devil in black had called his name. It was clearly no time for cute games. His life hung on a heartbeat, and Joey Puli knew it.

"I'm listening," said cold Judgment.

"Okay, I work here," Puli admitted weakly. "Messenger."

"Runner," Bolan corrected him.

"Sure, yeah. I pick up things and deliver things."

The death gaze flicked to the military medal that lay on the desk. "Pick that up and deliver it, then," the icy voice commanded.

A grin engulfed the terror of the runner's face as he replied, "Sure, man. Anything you say. Who gets it?"

"Oliveras gets it."

The grin shrank. "I'm not sure I know—"

"You know," Bolan told him. "And I'll know when he gets it. If he doesn't get it, Joey, then it's yours to die with."

"He'll get it," the guy said in a choked voice.

"Take off," Bolan quietly commanded.

Puli snatched the medal from the desk and bolted from the room. Bolan went immediately to the wall safe and transferred its contents to his pouch—then lost no time getting out of there himself.

6

Minutes later the Executioner was at a darkened window of a high-rise hotel near Ala Wai Harbor. It was a carefully preselected "fire base" with an unobstructed view of another high-rise building far down the beach. A gleaming Weatherby Mark IV mounted in a swivel tripod shared that window with the marksman. The impressive weapon was equipped with a 20-power scope, a Startron model especially designed for night targeting. In the scope's field of vision, another window was framed—nearly a thousand meters downrange. This one was brightly lighted and revealed one half of a sizable room—a luxury pad, even for Waikiki. Nothing human was moving through that field of vision, however, as Bolan checked and doublechecked the calibrated range marks of the crosshairs. He grunted with satisfaction, doggedly ran another calculation on the trajectory graph which had been laboriously set up for this mission, then he checked once again the lateral stops on the swivel mount.

Finally, fully satisfied with his preparations, Bolan bent once again to the eyepiece of the scope and patiently waited.

That was the name of the game now. Wait. For targets.

The whole thing now depended entirely upon Joey Puli.

The object of Bolan's concern was at that moment checking in to the swank diggings of Frank Oliveras, the reputed heroin king of the islands. "Listen," he reported urgently into the house phone, "this is Joey Puli. You know. Angliano. Listen—he just got smeared. Know what I mean? I got to see Mr. Oliveras damn quick. His life might depend on it."

Puli smirked at the security man and handed the

telephone to him. A moment later he was passed through to the elevator to begin the quick ascent to the upper levels. Both hands in his pockets, the little runner mentally rehearsed his speech to the great man while nervously fingering the outlines of the military medal.

He stepped from the elevator and into the rough hands of a reception committee, by whom he was frisked, then unceremoniously led into the apartment and shoved onto a chair in a small reception hall. The men promptly withdrew, leaving him there alone. The room was a mere cubicle, windowless, with a massive door at either end. The hard chair on which he sat was the only piece of furniture. A heavy mirror was set into the wall opposite the chair. Puli gazed into the mirror, then quickly averted his eyes as a chill seized the nape of his neck with some instinctive awareness that eyes other than his own were staring back at him from that "mirror." He fidgeted, lit a cigarette, put it out, returned both hands to his pockets —then, on impulse, he produced the medal and began examining it.

Immediately, the inner door opened and two stony-faced men entered. Torpedoes, these—it was stamped all over them.

Puli was roughly frisked again and one of the men snatched the medal.

"Hey, wait," the islander complained weakly. "That's for—"

"What's your name again?" asked the one who had taken the medal.

"Puli, Joey. I work for—I *worked* for—"

"What do you want here?"

"I got to see Mr. Oliveras. It's okay, I'm connected.

I worked for Angliano. That's what I got to see Mr. Oliveras about. Angles is dead."

"So what?"

Puli's gaze shifted nervously between the two men. "So I was there, that's so what. The guy blasted his head away." Uncomfortable eyes fell to the bull's-eye cross which was resting on the torpedo's palm. "He left that behind."

The men exchanged glances. The one with the medal said, "He left you, too."

"Yeah," Puli said, shuddering.

"Why?"

The little guy shuddered again. "I guess he figured I wasn't worth the price of a bullet."

The silent torpedo snickered coldly. The other said, "Baby-sit him, Charley," and departed.

"Sit down," the other sneered.

Puli returned to the chair.

A full minute passed—a very uncomfortable minute for Joey Puli, under the glassy gaze of his "baby sitter." Then the voice of the other man came from a speaker concealed somewhere in the wall: "Charley. Meet us in the office."

The visitor was escorted through a succession of darkened rooms, across a small garden-terrace patio, and into "the office." It was a large, oblong room with two entire walls of glass, obviously situated at the corner of the building, providing a spectacular view of both the beach area and the open sea. A huge mahogany desk was set across the corner, between the windows. Someone was seated at that desk, but Puli was looking directly into the bright glow of a desk lamp which was angled his way, and he could see only an indistinct form back there.

A rasping voice from that direction asked, "What'd you say your name was?"

"Joey Puli. Are you Mr. Oliveras?"

"Shut up!"

"Yessir."

"You just tell what I ask you."

"Yessir."

"What's this about Angliano?"

"He's dead."

"Why?"

Puli continued to gaze stoically into the blinding lamp as he explained, "I'd just brought in the evening receipts. Mr. Angliano was putting them in the safe when this guy came busting in. He was a—God, I don't know how to describe him. He wasn't no street-corner junkie, that's for sure. Big tall guy. Black gun with a silencer—and he sure knew what to do with it. Come to think, he was black all over. I mean, his clothes and everything, not his skin. White man. Didn't say anything, just raised that black gun and put a bullet between Mr. Angliano's eyes. Then he threw that medal on the desk and turned the gun on me. I talked him out of it. But he got Tommy Dragon before he came in—I mean, into the office. Tommy was on door duty. I saw him laying there with his brains oozing out, and I knew right away this guy was kill crazy. Anyway, I just cooled it, and—"

"What kind of medal, Joey?" the man at the desk rasped.

"Some kind of soldier's medal. The guy took it away from me, the guy that—"

"A marksman's medal."

"Is that what it is?"

"You didn't know that?"

"No sir, I never was in the army. I don't know—"

10

"Who'd this guy say he was?"

"What guy? You mean the guy that took it or—"

"Dummy! You're a dummy!"

"Sir?" Things were getting out of hand. Joey Puli was beginning to sweat. This was crazy. These people were pure crazy.

"Did you really expect to get away with this kind of shit?"

"What? Aw no, no! You got me wrong, Mr. Oliveras! I'm giving you this straight on the level! What d'you think I did? You think I did this myself and just made up a story? You think I'd come *here* after I done something like *that?*"

"Shut up!"

"Well, I just—"

Someone stepped up from the rear and slapped Puli with an open hand across the back of his head. The runner caught his breath and closed his mouth with a snap.

The rasping voice from the desk was telling him, "You know how many times this has been tried, dummy? You know how many punks have tried cashing in on this guy's reputation? You think we just automatically start shaking and shitting if somebody just says the guy's in town? What do you take us for? You must take me for some—shit, you don't even think you have to mention the *name!* You just come dancing in here with this goddam piece of *junk* in your hand, and I'm gonna kiss you like a hero!"

"*What* name?" Puli moaned. "I don't know what you're talking about! The guy came in and shot up the joint! He gave me the damned medal and told me to bring it here! That's all I know!"

"You're a *punk!* So now you're saying he *told* you to bring it here!"

"Yessir, I thought I said that already. I didn't want —listen, I was scared to come here. But the guy said it was my only out. He said I either bring the thing here and give it to you or I die with it myself. I don't even know what's going on, I swear."

"This so-called guy says you're to bring it to me? By name, he says *me?*"

"If you're Mr. Oliveras, yessir, that's right. He says you."

"Who'd he say *he* was?"

"God, sir, he didn't say. He acted like he didn't *need* to say. He just says I should take it to Oliveras or die with it myself."

"Your*self?*"

"Yessir."

"You mean, like, instead of *my*self!"

"Well . . . maybe. I don't r'member. God, look, I'm standing there in Mr. Angliano's brains. The guy turns the gun on me." The little runner was beginning to crumble under the strain. His eyes rolled as he continued, "Hey, God, you gotta see this guy to believe him. I was scared *shit!* I mean I never been so scared in my life! You gotta *see* this guy! You never *saw* such *eyes!* And cold—listen, that guy was solid ice. He—"

"Big guy, you say?" asked a calm voice behind him. It was the torpedo who'd taken the medal.

Puli half-turned to the sound of that voice as he replied, "Yessir, very tall. Big, but not fat. I mean— across the shoulders, the chest—powerful, big, but— and all dressed in black. Eyes like . . . like . . ."

A heavy sigh came from the desk to punctuate Puli's awed search for words. "What do you think, Oscar?" Oliveras rasped.

"It sounds straight, sir," the torpedo called Oscar replied.

"Sounds like Bolan to me," said the other.

Something highly discomfiting was finally coming together in Joey Puli's mind. One knee buckled under that onslaught of revelation and he nearly toppled over. "Oh God!" he moaned. "Was that—was that . . . ?"

"You saying you didn't know?"

"I swear I didn't know," Puli weakly insisted. "I didn't finger you, Mr. Oliveras. The guy did, he already knew. He says, 'Pick that up and deliver it to Oliveras.' You just gotta believe that. I didn't even know who the guy was. He just says—"

"Shut up!"

"Yessir." Puli steeled himself for another blow from the rear, but none came. He stood with shoulders slumped, staring at his toes in abject contrition.

From the desk: "Oscar."

"Yes, sir."

"You better check this out. Not direct. Call the guy over at HPD. Tell him to verify this. I want to know damn quick."

The guy moved to a telephone somewhere to the rear.

"Charley."

"Sir."

"Put this kid on ice until we know what's going on here."

The escorting torpedo grabbed Puli's arm and spun him around, moving him out. Oscar was standing at a small table near the window, speaking into a telephone. From the corner of his eye Puli saw a huge bulk of a man moving away from the desk in the corner.

Then all hell broke loose.

13

The big picture window at the north wall popped and vibrated as something sizzled into that room and exploded into the face of Puli's escort, jerking the guy like a rag doll and sending pieces of him spraying everywhere. The window popped again before the little runner could fully comprehend what had occurred, and with that one the guy at the telephone was flung across the room in another shower of blood.

Puli instinctively hit the floor and hugged it as the window continued to erupt and a seemingly eternal fusillade of heavy bullets demolished everything within reach.

Some other guys came charging in, only to be screamed back by Oliveras who—Puli noted—was also as flat on the floor as his huge girth would allow.

And when it was over, the silence was even more ominous than the preceding chaos. Two men lay gruesomely dead almost at Joey Puli's outstretched fingertips. The entire room was a wreck. Puli was aware that his fingers were stiff and aching, and that he had wet himself.

Then, behind him, the quivering rasp of Frank Oliveras' voice sounded off with a seemingly endless stream of solemn obscenities.

That desk back there was splintered beyond belief. It was a miracle that Oliveras was alive to cuss about it.

And another miracle was quickly borne in on Joey Puli's trembling awareness—he, Joey Puli, was a very, very lucky man. He had lived through two hits by the most fearsome son of a bitch in Puli's dark world.

The Executioner had come to Hawaii.

And the bastard was on the rampage.

2: Moving Up

The evening was just beginning to swing at the Oahu Cove, a gaudy supper club which was operated in conjunction with the apartment complex owned by Frank Oliveras. Headlining the entertainment at the club for "the third big week" was the man who'd become accustomed to being billed as "the hottest comic in the land," Tommy Anders. It was the first time since Vegas that these two trails had crossed, and Bolan had mixed feelings about this occasion. It was nice to see old friends, sure—but friends had an uncomfortable facility for becoming liabilities to a one-man army; Bolan had learned to shun personal contacts whenever possible. This one seemed necessary, however.

He had changed into casual evening wear and was seated at a back table at Oahu Cove as the comic concluded his first show of the night. Anders was a satirist and had come a long way poking fun at the nation's ethnic sensitivities. He hadn't changed a bit since Vegas.

"I'm not no ethnician—I'm just a lost wop without a Godfather—but I gotta say it, these people here in Five-Oh state are beating the devil with his own stick. It's a majority of minorities here, and I don't believe these people even know the difference anymore.

15

They've got a Jap in the state house, a Chinaman in Congress, and a Polynesian in their supreme court. How ridiculous can you get? They're men! Every one of them. Chauvinist minority pigs! Why the hell don't they send some hula girls to Congress? A little grass shack up on Capitol Hill—what's wrong with that? I'm telling you—I'm not no ethnician, but . . . Prostitution used to be legal, back when this state was a territory. That came in somewhere between the missionaries and the Honolulu Hilton—back during those great old days of WASP rule, remember Pearl Harbor, and Mamie Stover. Now that they got home rule with a majority of minorities running things, the only lay a guy can get on this island is the one they hang around your neck when you arrive. Everything's illegal now. You can't even pee on the beach without getting fined. Pers'nally I don't care. Like I say, I'm not no ethnician—and all this law and order sets things up perfectly for *my* people. I don't care who they put in politics in this country as long as everybody understands that it's the Italians who are really running things. This is Tommy Anders, also known in dark alleys as Guiseppe Androsepitone, proudly saying good night and may the Godfather smile on you all."

The little guy left the stage with a good hand, then reappeared for a brief bow as the curtain raised behind him and a troop of westernized hula dancers took over.

A few minutes later he was sliding onto the chair opposite Bolan, his eyes dancing with restrained excitement and his breath coming hard. "God Jesus, it *is* you," he exclaimed in a muffled voice. "What the *hell* are you doing on this island!"

Bolan grinned and took the comic's hand in a warm grasp. "Same as you, I'd guess," he replied, assuming more than he actually knew. It seemed a pretty safe bet, though, that Anders had been involved in a federal undercover operation while at Las Vegas. "Which way are the hounds running?"

Anders chuckled as he signaled the waiter. "In circles, right now, I'd say. The word is sweeping the island like the big waves up at Makaha. I figured it was just a wild rumor but . . . well, here you are, right?"

The waiter was waiting. Bolan covered his glass with the palm of his hand and shook his head in response to the lifted eyebrows of his friend. Anders ordered a drink. The waiter departed. The little guy picked it up again right on the beat. "I got your envelope backstage just now and I thought, God Jesus, it's true, the goddam guy is really here and storming. Man, you do love suicide details, don't you. How do you figure to get off this damn island?"

"Maybe I won't need to," Bolan said, smiling. He lit a cigarette while Anders stared at him, waiting for more than that.

"That's a hell of an attitude," Anders replied presently. "I thought you always had these things so damn well planned."

"Just the openers, Anders. The end can take care of itself. What do you have going here?"

"Third and last big week," the comic said, smiling sourly.

"Baloney."

The guy laughed out loud. "Okay. I guess I owe you honesty, at the very least. Right now you're seated in company property."

Bolan said, "I know. I just hit upstairs a little while ago."

The comic's face went blank. "You did what?"

"I gave Oliveras a little sneak preview of things to come."

"When was this?"

Bolan glanced at his watch. "Little less than an hour ago."

Anders rolled his eyes at that. He glanced nervously about them as he said, "So that's what all the flap was about. I didn't connect it with the other rumors— mainly because I just couldn't see you committing yourself to this small arena. Well . . . after Vegas, I guess nothing should surprise me where you're concerned. But you'd better get on your bicycle and pedal the hell away from this joint, right quick. This whole damn place is an armed camp. I could point out to you ten very unfriendly torpedoes without leaving this table. And they—"

"I have them spotted," Bolan said quietly.

The comic's eyes warmed and a smile worked at his lips. "I'll bet you do, at that. Tell me something else, phantom. How come *they* never have *you* spotted?"

Bolan chuckled drily. "Dead men do not draw pictures. The others are working at role images. You should know all about that game. But I don't play it their way."

Anders was giving the big man a searching gaze. "Yeah," he said. "Who'd you hit?"

"Couple of Ollie's boys. Right now I don't want the man himself. The trail ends at him. I need the next connection, the next man high. You know who that might be?"

Anders shook his head. "You hear rumors all the time, but they're not worth a damn. The only word I can believe says that Oliveras himself is the top card."

Bolan said, "It doesn't fit. Too many outrankers coming in. It's been a regular tourist flow the past few months. Rodani from Detroit. Topacetti from Chicago. Benvenuti from St. Louis and Pensa from

18

Cleveland. New York has sent Dominick and Flora—Boston, Tommy Odono. That's too much firepower for a guy like Oliveras to crew. He's a junk runner, period. Something bigger than junk is brewing on these islands. What is it?"

The comic shook his head with a doleful grimace. "Nobody knows."

"That's why you're here?"

"One reason, yeah."

"What's the other?"

"You remember those Ranger Girls."

Bolan flinched. Sure, he remembered. How could he forget? "I saw Toby in Detroit a while back," he replied.

"I hear you saw Georgette, also," Anders said quietly.

Sure. Bolan had given the Canuck bodybomb a merciful death. "I did," he said.

The comic was staring into his drink. "This is a high-risk business," he muttered. "We all know that. We accept it as a fringe benefit when we take the job."

Bolan said, "Yeah."

"Smiley accepted that, too."

Smiley Dublin, sure—the beautiful kid who, even in Vegas, seemed to have lost all her smiles long ago. "What are you saying?" Bolan growled.

Anders sighed. "We're looking for her."

"I see. And the trail gets cold right here."

"Yeah. It ended here four weeks ago."

Bolan closed his eyes, very tightly, fighting back a surge of emotion. He was trying to call up a vision of a divine body, saucy head and elfin face, a lovely kid with talent enough to storm the world but also possessing guts enough to tackle its nether regions. And all he could summon up was a pitiful wreck of a

19

human being who pleaded only for death's release from a back porch of hell in Detroit one terribly dismal night.

"What'd you say?" Anders asked.

Bolan had not been aware that he'd said anything. But the moment passed as he replied, "I said that's too long."

"Maybe not. I keep hearing whispers."

"Like what?"

"You hear of a Chinese guy called Chung?"

Bolan nodded. "Local muscle."

"Right, with full franchise to flex it whenever and wherever. Has a place over on the big island, secret place. The whispers say that Chung keeps political prisoners over there."

"For what purpose?" Bolan wondered aloud.

Anders shrugged. "Maybe for fun and games, maybe for something else."

"How many are working this with you?"

"Right now, just me," Anders replied, sighing. "The local authorities are clued in, but only at the very highest levels. We're afraid to show a hand at this stage of things."

"You want me to butt out?" Bolan asked quietly.

"No. You're here, you may as well wade right in. The water's warm already. Bring it to a boil. Maybe something good will float to the top."

"Okay." Bolan placed money on the table and got to his feet.

"Where're you headed?" Anders inquired, tight-lipped.

"Upstairs."

The comic sighed. "I know better than to say anything about that. But you're crazy, you know. Maybe you got in there once, but you'll never do it twice in the same night."

Bolan smiled and again shook hands. "Great to see you again, Anders. I'll be in touch."

"Sure."

"If you have any silent friends in the woodwork, now's the time to tell me."

"I told you, there's no one."

Bolan smiled again and went out.

He took a small arcade to the main lobby and approached the security desk, scowling. A uniformed guard greeted him pleasantly enough, but the guy was obviously edgy.

Bolan allowed his shoulder harness to show briefly as he opened his coat to produce an official badge wallet which he flashed at the guy and immediately returned to his pocket. "Fourteenth floor," he said brusquely. "Disturbance report. Your people check it out?"

"Well, sure," the guard replied, his smile still hanging in there. "I called in the okay on that nearly an hour ago." He snorted as he explained, "Damn flock of birds flew right against a window up there."

"I'll have to check it out," Bolan insisted. He snared the building register and signed in.

The guard was protesting, "Well, wait, I better call . . ." as Bolan moved on to the elevators.

The guy had the phone to his ear as Bolan stepped into the car and punched off. There would be a reception awaiting him up there, sure. He sprung the Beretta and threaded the silencer aboard, then closed his left fist around a spare clip and waited for that door to slide open.

He was going in cold, with only the haziest idea concerning the lay of that hellground up there, and

21

less than an hour after a hard-punch hit on the same joint.

A hellground in the sky, sure—that's what it would be.

So what was new? There was nothing *new* between life and death, not for a guy like Mack Bolan.

All corners of hell smelled the same.

3: Blitzing

Four men were waiting for him in the small lobby at the fourteenth floor, but they obviously were not perpared for a blitz-in. It was a "cop set" of studied looseness—one guy idly shuffling papers at a tiny desk near the elevator, another seated casually in an over-stuffed chair along the wall, a matched pair lounging against a door at the far end, above which was mounted a closed-circuit television camera.

Hardsite security, sure. But not hard enough.

Bolan exploded into the lobby with the Beretta singing, the first round finding headbone at the desk and sending the paper shuffler toppling backward, round two arching wallward and punching the lounger into a sideways dive, chair and all.

The lightning one-two caught the whole set with reflexes frozen or dead. Rounds three and four spat across that small lobby to nail the two guys at the door before stunned nerves could react. The fifth round shattered the television camera and the rest of the clip tore the locking mechanism out of the door to the inner sanctum.

Bolan was ejecting the spent clip and clicking in the replacement as he moved swiftly into the "cool room" where earlier Joey Puli had awaited his audience with the boss of Oahu. Only a few heartbeats

23

had elapsed since the man from death erupted from that elevator. He was moving on tight, blitzing numbers which would make utter failure of the slightest hesitancy. There was therefore no lost motion as he entered the security cubicle and instantly read the situation there.

The inner door was of the heavy, security-interlock type—perhaps even electronically sealed. Bolan wasted no precious seconds on that door. Without breaking stride, he seized the wooden chair which had last accommodated Puli and heaved it into the mirrored wall. It kept right on going, taking a large area of the wall with it. Bolan dived into the wreckage, with no idea of what he was leaping into other than a flash impression of scrambling bodies in electric reaction.

The security cell was dimly lit, small, unfurnished except for a couple of stools and a control console. Three men were in there: one now lying on the floor and groaning in the wreckage, another backed against the wall and waving a gun, the other moving quickly toward a door.

The Beretta coughed in instant reaction to the most immediate challenge. The hardman at the wall died with eyes bugging and weapon firing reflexively into the ceiling. The guy at the door snapped off a wild shot as he disappeared into another room. The one on the floor was dazedly trying to find a path to his weapon when a Parabellum whanger opened his pathway to hell instead.

Bolan assimilated the security layout of that fourteenth floor suite with a quick glance at the electronic console. It was exactly as his intelligence probes had indicated: Oliveras was almost paranoid in his security precautions. Every door in the joint was interlocked through this master panel.

The blitz artist paused only long enough to energize the master unlock control before charging on through the doorway. He reached that point just as the third man was sprinting through an arched doorway at the far end of a larger room. The Beretta coughed in pursuit, her zinging little missile overtaking the prey and punching him forward in a face-down slide to nowhere.

The guy could have been headed for only one point. Bolan followed that trail to its logical end, a room at the outside wall protected by a massive door with ornate hardware.

The door was several inches ajar but swinging closed when Bolan got there. He hit it at full gallop and went right on through. A small guy at the opposite side was caught in the backswing; he was stumbling backwards, falling, a snubbed .38 in one paw discharging into the floor. A Parabellum sizzler exploded into the guy's face as Bolan ran over him and moved on into a large, lavishly decorated room.

It was a bedroom, and more, sporting a circular bed outfitted with a variety of kinky devices. There was also a bar, a sunken bath, a small gym in one corner, an efficiency kitchen, a miscellany of overstuffed furniture. Oliveras evidently did most of his living here in this one room. But not at the moment.

Joey Puli was the only occupant of the room. He was tied to a chrome kitchen chair near the bed. His mouth was bleeding, his face puffy and discolored. The little Hawaiian stared at the new arrival with haunted eyes and muttered, "Look at what you got me into."

Bolan growled, "Where's Oliveras?"

Those glazed eyes shifted to the far side of the room. "Hiding in the closet."

Indeed he was. Wearing silk pajamas and holding a

snifter of brandy as though it were a gun, dulled eyes flicking in search of some way out of the box, the Lord of Oahu greeted Judgment with a despairing groan.

From two paces out, Bolan flipped a death medal into the brandy glass and quietly announced, "There you go."

The fat man leaned weakly against a rack of five-hundred-dollar suits and groaned, "Wait. Let's be sure about this."

"I'm sure," Bolan said coldly. "Kiss it goodbye, guy."

"Wait. Please. We can work this out. Anything you want. Just name it, you got it. I'm a rich man. I can give—"

Bolan stepped back and commanded, "Get out of there."

Oliveras grabbed the door jamb and pulled himself upright, then all but fell into the room. The glass dropped and rolled across the floor, spilling its contents.

"I'm a sick man," Oliveras whimpered.

Bolan shoved him to a chair opposite Puli as he replied to that. "Not for long," he assured the guy. "Unless you know some way to make me very happy."

"Whatever you say. I swear. Anything."

The guy desperately wanted to live. How desperately, though?

Bolan quietly asked him, "Why all the mobbing-up here in Hawaii?"

"I don't know anything about that," Oliveras muttered.

"Then you're not going to make me very happy." Bolan turned a frigid gaze toward Puli. "You want to do the honors, Joey?"

26

"Just untie me and then watch me," the Hawaiian huffed.

"Wait a minute," Oliveras said quickly. "You mean people like Dominick and Flora?"

"Yeah. People like that."

"I'm not really in that. Protocol says, sure—they check in with me then go on their own way. But I don't know what they're doing here."

"Who's sending them?"

"Well—you know."

"Tell me so I'll know for sure."

"The old men."

"Which old men?"

"You know." The fat man was fidgeting uncomfortably, eyes downcast, studying his hands. "The councilmen."

La Commissione. Sure, Bolan knew that. But these people had the fear of *omerta* born into them. Such innate defenses had to be approached properly.

"You're telling me nothing, guy!" Bolan declared in an icy voice. "My time is up. So is yours."

"Wait! This is level! I'm nothing to those people— *nothing!* And they *tell* me nothing!"

"So what should I *wait* for, Oliveras?"

Those troubled eyes rolled upwards and the big man shuddered under the onslaught of conflicting emotions. "Chung," he sobbed, the voice barely audible.

"What about Chung?"

Another shudder, then: "He's the center man."

"What's he centering?"

"I swear I don't know."

The Beretta sighed without warning. The huge bulk of the boss of Oahu corkscrewed off the chair to land in a seated position on the floor. Joey Puli's eyes flared

27

wide, then closed above gritting teeth. Blood was pumping in bright spurts from a rip in Oliveras' shoulder.

The guy's face was a total blank, head swiveled in stunned contemplation of the gushing wound. A huge hand flopped heavily to that area and fat fingers tried to stanch the flow.

Bolan's stiletto whipped through the sashcord that held Puli in his chair. "Your turn, Joey," Bolan said as he freed the little guy's hands. "You want to carve him or shoot him?"

"Wait!" shrieked the bleeding man from the floor. "Chung has a place over on Hawaii, the big island. Something big, something really hot! I don't know where it is, exactly. In some valley, away from things. Big place!"

Bolan made no comment to that. He was staring at Puli. "Well?"

"The knife," Puli replied weakly, on to the game now and bravely trying to carry his end of it. "I'll take him a piece at a time."

That was the end of Oliveras' *omerta*—the sacred oath of silence. He struggled to his knees, babbling in the release. There was not much to be made from it in the form of hard intelligence, but Bolan went away from there convinced that he now knew at least as much as Oliveras himself knew about the "big thing" in Hawaii. He also went away with pretty good directions to the next front.

They left the boss of Oahu kneeling drunkenly in his own blood on his bedroom floor, and Bolan and Puli withdrew through the carnage of an Executioner hard hit, then descended to the main lobby via the elevator.

They paused at the guard desk while Bolan tersely

reported to a confused security cop. "It wasn't birds, guy. You'd better call Honolulu Central and tell them to bring a meat bus with them."

Then they moved unchallenged through the lobby and out the door on the beach side.

Puli, speaking stiffly through mangled lips, marveled, "You are something else, mister. Please don't ever get mad at me. Or are you, anyway?"

Bolan chuckled and told his new admirer, "You're not the enemy, Joey."

"Thank God," the little guy replied. And he said a silent prayer for all who were.

4: The Big One

Greg Patterson, the lieutenant from homicide, stepped out of the elevator at the fourteenth floor and into a slaughterhouse. Detectives Tinkamura and Kale, who had arrived at the scene some minutes earlier, quickly came forward to greet him, picking their way carefully through the blood-spattered disaster zone.

"What is this—bonus night?" Patterson grunted. He was a large man, early middle age, tough, one-hundred-percent cop.

"There's more inside," Tinkamura reported soberly.

"All told, ten," said Detective Kale.

"Oliveras?" Patterson asked, almost hopefully.

"Naw," Kale replied. "The medics took him away about five minutes ago. Shoulder wound, an easy one. He lost some blood. That's about all, except for fifty or sixty pounds of dignity."

The lieutenant had moved over to stand astride a grotesquely twisted corpse and was peering into the mutilated face. "Is that Wheels Morgan?" he asked nobody in particular.

Tinkamura replied. "Could be. I could even hope so. Couldn't you?"

"They're all head hits," Kale volunteered. "Very messy."

30

"*All* of them?" Patterson growled.

"Yeah. Somebody ran wild in here, that's for sure. Somebody who got inside easy past all this security without being challenged. Not until he'd penetrated the—"

"Hold it!" Patterson snapped. "Aren't you assuming a lot? Why do you say *he*? Why not *they*?"

Detective Kale grimaced. "The medical examiner came in with us. His quick guess is one weapon, one man. Except for the two at the southwest corner, and that didn't come at the same time. It came earlier. A high-powered rifle, for sure. Also, they're stuffed into weighted bags. Awaiting burial at sea, I'd guess. So—"

"So shit you've lost me," Patterson said quietly.

Tinkamura smiled sourly as he updated the lieutenant. "Kale and I responded to a gunfire report at 902, down at Ala Wai Tower. Several occupants of the upper floors complained that someone was firing a rifle up there. We didn't find anything—not there, not then. But at about that same time there was a disturbance report from this building—a big commotion on the fourteenth floor, this one. It was never dispatched for investigation because the building security people called in an okay. We get this later, see. Said a bunch of birds flew right through a glass wall. Well, you know, that's not too far out. It does happen. So—"

"Yeah, yeah," Patterson interrupted impatiently. "So anyway . . ."

"So at about ten, one hour later, an alarm comes in from the security people here—a bell ringer. Patrol unit responded, took one look from the elevator there, then called us in. We took one look at this mess and I guess the same thought clanged our minds at the same time. We made a beeline to the south side of the building and sure as hell, there it was. Our nine o'clock gunfire report."

"Yeah?"

"Yeah. Some hot cock was shooting from over half a mile away, and he tore hell out of everything at this southwest window, including the unlucky heads of Oscar Meyer Weeni and Charley Boy Tellevecci. Head hits, I mean, from the Ala Wai Tower. I never—"

"Now hold it!" the lieutenant protested. "I'm not riding with you boys, for some reason. Don't tell me, dammit. Show me."

Several minutes later, the one-hundred-percent cop had been shown all he cared to see for one duty day. He was in the Oliveras bedroom, staring down at the very messy remains of one Trigger John Minelli, who had carried the reputation of being the fastest gun in the islands.

The medical examiner, a tired-looking man with nervous eyes, had just declared, "It's going to be one of those nights at the morgue."

"Yeah," Patterson quietly agreed.

"Ten all at once. We M. E.'s ought to have a union. We'd protest—"

"Twelve," Patterson corrected.

"Yeah, we'd—twelve?"

The lieutenant handed over a sheet of note paper. "Two more at this address. And I'll bet I can tell you before you get there. Head hits—same weapon, same man."

The M. E. muttered something unintelligible and ambled away.

"What was that?" Kale asked the lieutenant.

"That was Paul Angliano and his shadowman. Or so the report says. A vice detective called it in. I got it on my way here."

"Hey, hey," Tinkamura commented thoughtfully. "We got a drug war."

"I'm betting we got more than that," Patterson growled. He was slowly pacing off the room, head bent, eyes alert. "What is Oliveras saying?"

"Nothing at all," Kale replied, glancing at his partner. "We've put a hold on him at the hospital. We'll try to get a statement before we check in."

"Do that," Patterson said absently. He had dropped to one knee to examine something on the carpet near the closet door. An empty brandy snifter lay nearby.

Kale said, "We'll get the lab men to dust that glass, Lieutenant."

"Do that," Patterson again replied, his mind obviously focused elsewhere. He had produced a handkerchief, which he wrapped about his hand to carefully lift a small object from the floor.

"What do you have there?" Tinkamura inquired.

"The answer, I think," Patterson replied in a strained voice.

"How much of an answer?"

"Too damned much, maybe." The lieutenant extended the linen-wrapped hand so that his junior officers could see what was lying there, a metallic object in the shape of an iron cross with a bull's eye at its center.

"Hell, I should have known," Tinkamura declared in hushed tones.

"That guy wouldn't be *here*," Kale observed, scoffing at the idea.

"It looks like he is," Patterson said quietly. "You said head hits at a half a mile? That's no trick for a guy like Bolan. Who else can you think of who might pull a stunt like that, then waltz right in to mop it up?"

33

Tinkamura muttered, "Tell the doc he better join that union quick."

"I still can't believe it," Kale said, obviously not wanting to. His gaze shifted to a chrome chair near the bed. "Who was tied to that chair? I believe we have separate incidents here. Put together, sure, it looks like one thing. Take it all apart, it's something else entirely."

The lieutenant glanced at a uniformed officer at the door. "Bring that lobby guard in," he instructed.

The security cop was ushered in carrying a registry book under his arm, gazing uneasily about the large room and stepping carefully around the corpse at the doorway.

"Who came up here tonight?" Patterson asked him.

The guard handed over the register as he reported, "Only two, as you can see. The eight-fifty entry was a kid in his early twenties. Looked like a beach boy. He was cleared by phone and I sent him on up. That's all, except for Sergeant Nalob there—the next entry— see? He was up here for just a few minutes. Came back down with the Puli kid in tow. The kid was all beat up. I'd just received a call from the thirteenth floor. Lady said she heard a couple of gunshots. Well, I knew Nalob was up here. I didn't know what to think—but then I got to worrying maybe he was in trouble. Finally decided to call it in when here comes Nalob and the beach boy. He instructed me to call and I did."

"You said a *couple* of gunshots?" Patterson pressed. "That's all? A couple?"

"Yes, sir. Mrs. Rogers in 13-A, that's exactly how she said it, a couple of gunshots."

"Silencer," Tinkamura muttered.

Patterson was staring quizzically at the security cop. "This guy Nalob. What's he look like?"

The cop looked suddenly flustered. "Don't you know him? He showed identification. Big fella, well over six feet. About two hundred pounds. I'd say, late twenties, early thirties. Dark hair, medium skin. Blue eyes, I believe—yeah, blue and very piercing. He looks holes through you."

Kale said, "I don't know any Nalob."

"Wait outside," Patterson instructed the guard, returning his register. "Hang on to that book."

The guy went out gladly.

"Well, there you are," Patterson declared, eyes on the marksman's medal.

"The description fits, all right," Tinkamura agreed.

"Take that guard down to Central," the lieutenant instructed his officers. "Let's see what the artist can do."

"Right. And just for the hell of it, I'll check out this Nalob. But I never heard of any—"

Patterson stopped him with a clucking chuckle and said, "You still hung up on that? You won't find a Nalob in the department, Tink. *Nalob* is *Bolan* spelled backward."

A brief silence fell upon the gathering, then Tinkamura laughed loudly. "How 'bout that guy!" he said admiringly.

Kale's action was quite the reverse. "Crazy," he declared, voice muffled. "It is, it's crazy. He must know we can seal him on this island. He'll never get off alive!"

"You bet he won't," Patterson said grimly, closing his fist on the medal. "You boys stay here until the lab crew arrives. Then get that guard down to Central and let's get some composites." He'd already spun on

35

his toe and was marching from the room at a quick pace.

"You want us to report this?" Tinkamura called after the departing figure. "Set up an all-points?"

"I do not!" the lieutenant yelled back. "I'll handle it!"

Damn right he'd handle it. Greg Patterson was personally taking this little bombshell to market.

He meant to get the assignment, the prime spot.

And he intended to see to it, personally, that the most wanted man in the free world did not leave these islands a free man.

The one-hundred-percent cop was going to, by God or by otherwise, bag the big one. He was going to *get* Mack Bolan!

At about the same moment that Lieutenant Patterson was quitting the scene of carnage, the man called Chung was receiving a furtive visitor at his Oriental-style home in the Kalihi Valley, a few miles north of Honolulu.

The two men greeted each other in restrained tones and paced the edge of a lotus pond in the walled garden. Stiffly formal and making small talk, the visitor obviously uncomfortable, awaiting the signal that the official conversation might begin.

The host was a stocky, powerful-looking man of perhaps forty years. He wore only a terrycloth karate wraparound and sandals. The face was impassive, eyes hardly visible behind folds of hard flesh, black hair bristling in a severe crew cut.

The visitor was a Caucasian, fairly young, neatly attired in a conservative business suit, good looking. At the moment he was nervous, on edge—and with good reason. George Riggs was a cop.

36

Chung paused beside a small statue of the Buddha, struck a match on it, and lit a cigar. Then he told his visitor, "All right, George—you may report."

It was some sort of ritual. Riggs suspected that it had something to do with Chung's security. They always met in the garden. They always strolled the lotus pond, making small talk. Chung always struck the match and lit the cigar before any business got underway. And George Riggs always had the uncomfortable feeling that concealed eyes were following his every movement.

"Mack Bolan is on the island," he reported flatly, watching the other closely for reaction.

There was none. Chung took several pulls at the cigar before replying, "Is that fact or guess?"

"Fact, I'm afraid. I got a call at about nine o'clock from Oscar Weeni. He was telling me that some punk had brought over a marksman's medal from Paul Angliano's office. Said that Paul and his tagman were supposed to be dead, wanted me to check it out. I did, and they are. A slug in each head. While I was talking to Oscar, though, all hell broke loose over there. Right in the middle of a sentence, Oscar went *unghh* and that was the end of the conversation. I could tell that the phone hit the floor. And there was a hell of a commotion going on. No gunfire, none of that, but the sound of *incoming*. Know what I mean? Heavy slugs punching in from somewhere way out and just tearing hell out of everything. That lasted for just a few seconds, then the phone went dead. I tried to call back, kept getting a busy signal."

"Is Frank dead?"

"No. And I need to tell this the way it happened. Otherwise it gets very confusing. I walked around on eggshells for about five minutes, I guess, after the

37

telephone incident, then I hopped in my car and went over there. I didn't go in, though—just cruised past a couple of times. Saw no evidence of a police response. Figured the situation was in hand, and I didn't want to go barging in at a time like that. I was off duty. I went down to headquarters and nosed around. Nothing was on. So I called Frank's apartment again, and this time I got through. I talked to Trigger John. He said Frank was taking a bath to calm his nerves, that he was okay. He said Oscar and Charley Boy were dead, but it was being quieted. Said some guy with a fantastic eye, Bolan maybe, had parked away off somewhere and raked Frank's office with rifle fire—something, too, about some punk kid who worked for Angliano maybe helping to set it up for the rifleman. They still wanted me to verify the Angliano hit. So I went on over there. Some people saw me enter, so I had to straight it. I delayed as long as I could, then I called in the report and waited for the homicide detail to relieve me. When I went back past Frank's building there were official cars everywhere and cops running all around the place. I parked and went in for a closer look. Just as I got to the lobby, they were bringing Frank out on a stretcher. He's a lucky man, Chung. He caught only a flesh wound in the shoulder. I had a chance for only a couple of quiet words with him. He said I should tell you quick to look out—that it was Bolan, all right—that the guy hadn't been satisfied with the sharpshooter bit, that he'd come right on up there an hour later, past all that security, that he'd wiped out Frank's entire force."

"One man," Chung commented thoughtfully.

"Yeah."

"Single-handedly. A real American hero."

The cop lit a cigarette and blew the smoke in a

strong gust toward the lotus pond. "That's what they say about the guy, yeah. How much is truth and how much is myth is for someone else to say. But I've read all the official bulletins on the guy from the mainland. And let me tell you—even at seventy-five-percent myth, he's a dangerous son of a bitch."

"So I've heard. We get our bulletins too, you know."

"Yeah. Well, that's all I have. I thought you'd want to know."

"It seems quite enough," Chung mused. "Except . . ."

"Except what?"

"Why is Frank not as dead as the others?"

"I told you, he got lucky. A flesh wound in—"

"That's ridiculous!" Chung exploded.

"Well—okay, yeah. I see what you mean. So it wasn't luck."

"You'd better get back to Frank. Determine *why* he is alive. What price did he pay for that stupendous good luck? Once you have determined the truth, I think it best that Frank join his friends in the garden of silence."

"No, sir, not me," Riggs protested.

"You can set it up," Chung insisted. "Who else can? Better get to him before his lawyers begin swarming over that hospital with writs. Once he gets out . . ."

"I'm not going to do it, Chung," the cop said flatly. "I'm not in for that long a ride."

"You are in as far as I say you are," the Chinese said unemotionally. "If you wish to be a hero, go ahead. I'll see that you get a decent burial. As decent, at least, as your friend Frank's."

"*My* friend?" Riggs flipped his cigarette into the

lotus pond and went out of there without another word.

Chung remained beside the Buddha until the sound of the policeman's car faded into the distance; then he placed his cigar in the hands of the statue and brought his own hands together in a sharp clap.

Two Orientals in immaculate Western dress appeared immediately from the shadows at the wall, one of them grinning hugely.

"You heard?" Chung inquired.

"Yes," replied the grinning one. "So the big one has come."

"He has come," Chung affirmed. "And now we shall succeed where ten thousand Italians have failed. We shall behead the Executioner."

"And," added the grinner, "ten thousand Italians?"

"Oh, many more than that," Chung replied, chuckling. "But first the big one."

"It is done," said his companion, in perhaps the most optimistic pronouncement of the night. But the speaker had huge cause for optimism. Huge cause. Could eight hundred million Chinamen be wrong?

Perhaps they could.

As Chung and his companions linked arms and strolled casually toward the house, another shadow detached itself from the wall several yards downrange and moved silently across the "garden of peace."

The "big one" had indeed come. He had been there through the entire exchange.

5: The Task

Mack Bolan's declared war was with the Mafia. Yet he had known for some time that he was in fact battling more than *mafiosi*. The war fronts had been expanding continuously, almost from the beginning—broadening and splitting into diverse elements of an international power structure which, taken together, constituted an alliance of criminal influence which threatened to dominate the entire world.

Cosa di tutti Cosi was no idle dream. Literally translated, it meant "The Thing of all the Things"—or, loosely, The Big Thing. A bastardized stepchild of the original American idea, *La Cosa Nostra*—or, This Thing of Ours—the evolution from the old Italian-Sicilian *Mafia* to *Cosa di tutti Cosi* was on a scale comparable to the distance traveled from a Stone Age tribal council to the United Nations.

Bolan had long known that he was battling more than an accretion of American street hoodlums. Regardless of their present exalted status in the underworld hierarchy, guys like Augie Marinello and the other bosses who constituted the Cosa Nostra ruling council were still simply hoods. Success breeds success, however, and the fantastic wealth and power that had flowed almost unchecked for decades to this professional organization of criminals brought with it a capacity to attract those who naturally gravitate to the lure of easy wealth and unlimited power— with the result that a veritable *fourth world*, an international infrastructure of organized crime, inevitably came into existence.

This new shadow world was peopled not only with the traditional types of hoodlums, but also with "respectable" financiers, industrialists, politicians, brokers, traders, merchants, lawyers, lawmen, soldiers, athletes; the entire wide spectrum of human interests was well represented in that tidal wave of criminal avarice—and it was sweeping the world.

And, yes, Mack Bolan knew his enemies. They were the enemies of all honorable men everywhere. He had, however, attempted to limit his war, to contain it and direct it toward the most militant face of that enemy, to make war upon the armies and not upon the civilians—but those times did come when it was impossible to draw a line between soldier and civilian. Such a time had come in Texas. It had come in Haiti, in Detroit, in San Francisco and Seattle and, to a lesser degree, in the nation's capital and in Boston. Bolan had met the fourth worlders in many places and in many guises. And he had not hesitated to strike at those who cloaked themselves in respectability while feeding with the rest of the pack.

An entry in Bolan's personal war journal best illustrates the man's own understanding of the situation:

Despite what the media people are saying, I have never thought of myself as judge, juror, or avenging angel. I don't know what I am, and I do not even want to think too much about it. My gut knows, though, down there where rationalizations have no chance at it. I cannot co-exist peace-

42

fully with cannibals; that's the whole of it. I feel the same about the fellow travelers, the white-collar boys who've never had the smell of gunpowder on their hands. A cannibal without a spear, seated at the feast with his warrior brothers, is as guilty as any. As for my "simple solutions," let the moralizers and rationalizers come up with a complex solution that works and I will gladly hang up my guns. Until that time, I must keep on.

The war for Hawaii would present the severest test to this man's courage and resolve. He would be once again battling quite a bit more than a confederation of street hoods.

In Hawaii, the Executioner would be challenging the military arm of the fourth world. No more awesome an enemy had ever been faced by a man alone.

Minutes into the soft probe of the Chung headquarters in the Kalihi Valley of Oahu, Bolan was already receiving strong intimations to this effect. But the die was cast and the battle was on. There was no choice to make. Mack Bolan would keep on keeping on.

Against, even, eight hundred million Chinamen, if that be the task.

And, indeed, it was.

6: Kalihi

The Chung stronghold was situated on a couple of rugged, hilly acres near the head of the Kalihi Valley, in an area of dense vegetation and brooding mountain peaks. Beyond the mountains to the east lay Kaneohe Bay and that side of the island known as Windward, the sparsely settled section of Oahu. Just to the southeast soared magnificent Nuuanu Pali, the sheer cliff over whose precipice the eighteenth-century conqueror, Kamehameha the Great, drove thousands of Oahuan warriors to their deaths upon the jagged rocks below.

It had not always been paradise, no—not for everyone.

It was not going to be such for the mob, either—not if Mack Bolan had his say.

The Chung headquarters was officially billed as the Trans-Pacific Cultural Association. A seven-foot wall enclosed an artistic arrangement of gardens, pools, and fountains which themselves surrounded a modernistic glass and stone facsimile of Chinese architecture, a rather large building on two floors with small pagoda towers on its roofs.

Bolan had left his vehicle far to the rear to close on foot, getting the feel of the terrain and circling the estate at a wary distance—listening and watching and

44

reading the vibrations of that place from the high ground abutting it to the south.

A sensitive scout can soak in quite a bit from mere atmosphere. The atmosphere here was electric, pregnant with foreboding. It was a place of important, clandestine operations. The interior lighting of the house was muted, almost muffled despite the glass walls. Outside lighting was pinpointed via a battery of roof-mounted spotlights at each corner, in an arrangement which highlighted specific critical points while leaving much of the grounds darkened except for the pale wash of moonlight filtering through the broken clouds of the night. One of the pools had submerged lights, producing a peculiar glowing effect for the distant viewer. A bubbling fountain was spotlighted from the ground, sending dancing shadows to play upon a back wall.

Stonily silent men with infrared scanners and automatic weapons patrolled in pairs outside the walls, visible only to the professional eye and discernible only by the most patient surveillance. Bolan counted three paired patrols while quietly noting their routine and mentally mapping his route of penetration.

He was in skin-tight blacksuit, rigged for soft probe —packing only the silent Beretta in snap-draw shoulder rig, a nylon garrote, the trusty stiletto. Hands and face were blackened, feet softened in sure-grip rubber sneakers.

He made his move as an automobile approached along the drive, moving in behind its lights, then breaking for the wall from twenty yards out to thread the seam between the outer patrols. He hit the wall and was up and over in one fluid motion, dropping silently into a garden area, freezing there as a living component of the wall within hearing range of the vehicle gate, watching the automobile enter and turn slowly into the inner drive toward the house. It bore a single occupant, a man who was obviously well known by the gatemen. The vehicle swept out of sight behind a hedgerow and a moment later its head-lamps were extinguished.

A door opened and closed.

A male voice instructed an unseen greeter: "Tell the general I'm here. I'll be at the lotus pond."

Bolan moved on along the wall, then again froze as two men appeared from the direction of the house. They were walking rapidly and stealthily, and they appeared to be heading directly for Bolan.

He gave them room and much of his attention as he moved quietly on toward the corner of the wall and concealment beside a flowering bush. The pond with the submerged lights was now directly opposite his position. The two men from the house had blended into the shadows of the wall in the same area which Bolan had just vacated.

He was keeping those two in view and wondering about their intentions when a man in casual sports dress appeared on the flagstone path at the far side of the garden. The newcomer was immediately joined by another—a burly guy with bristling hair, wearing a karate wrap. The two stiffly shook hands and moved on toward Bolan's end of the garden, quietly conversing as they strolled.

Undoubtedly this was the visitor and "the general."

They halted beside a statue at the edge of the pond, and the conversation became a war report. The men at the wall were frozen in attitudes of close attention; one of them held a pistol with an elongated snout in a

46

firing stance, close-sighting across a clasped-elbow rest, targeting on one of the men at the pond—the visitor, no doubt.

It was all very interesting, as well as revealing. Bolan listened to the conversation, watched the visitor depart, then took interested note of the post-meeting critique by the three who remained. Personalities began sifting out there for Bolan. The tall man with the perpetual grin, an Oriental, ranked higher than the others. The one with the long pistol was obviously a low number—probably a bodyguard. The guy in the karate wrap was a power, all right, but he was not *the* power here.

As the three departed the garden, so too did Bolan. He broke cover directly in their wake and moved silently across to the house, becoming part of the larger shadow of a scudding cloud from windward, and made his entry almost in step with the others—but through a patio door to the rear.

Echoes of the VC: a little guy in black pajamas with a Mao collar rose from a chair directly in Bolan's path, a burper clutched to his chest and a cry of alarm boiling into his throat. The stiletto intercepted that cry before it reached vocalization, and snuffed it out forever. The sentry fell back into his chair with a dying gurgle. Bolan caught the falling weapon before it reached the floor and returned it to dead hands, positioned the sagging body in the chair, then went on.

He was in the darkened region of the building—the section which was evidently used for business purposes. He found offices, a conference room, a small gym with a reddishly glowing night light, then finally the goal of the probe: an executive suite.

And this was paydirt.

Double paydirt.

A small outer office opened to a larger room along the garden side. Oriental art decorated the walls and the smell of incense hung heavy in the air.

Beyond the doorway in the inner office an arresting figure in a transparent kimono was bent over a small lamp at the desk, going through some papers. It was a woman, totally nude beneath that wispy garment. Her back was to Bolan, and it was quite an appealing backside—a rather tall girl, strikingly formed, dark hair swept into an Oriental-type bun atop her head.

He moved on through the doorway.

She sensed the new presence in that room and turned to him with a rather glassy smile—a smile which instantly evaporated, to be replaced by a rather woeful march of conflicting emotions.

There were moments in the life of Mack Bolan that seemed like instant replays of past events. This was one of those.

The girl in the see-through kimono was the swinging Ranger Girl from Vegas, the show-stopper herself, the "missing" Smiley Dublin.

Bolan quietly closed the connecting door and gave her a long, close look, wondering if his own face were displaying that same sense of consternation that he was getting from Smiley's vibes. He took in the lay of the room with a single sweep of trained eyes, then returned his attention to the girl and took her into his arms for a brief but warm embrace.

She melted against him with a happy sigh and whispered, with moist lips at his ear, "Old thunder and lightning himself. How goes your war, Mr. Bolan?"

"Up till now, fine," he whispered back. "You ready to travel? I'm getting you out of here."

"In a pig's ass," she hissed. "Just get yourself out, and damn quick. Do you know what you're—oh no!" The girl pushed away from the embrace and locked gazes with the tall man in blackface. "Don't tell me you crashed in here on a rescue mission!"

Bolan shook his head. "Just probing. Others are looking for you, though, and with much concern."

"I couldn't chance a contact," she explained. "Look at me—I'm really connected. Tell them I'm very cozy and having a ball. Mack—I'm in something very big. Bigger than anyone can imagine. Now you butt the hell back out!"

Bolan moved quickly like a graceful cat, switching out the lamp and smoothly pushing the girl to the floor behind the desk.

"Hey, what—?"

"Shush!"

The door from the outer office opened and a shadowy figure leaned into the room. An overhead light clicked on and off, then the door closed again.

Bolan was lying partly atop the girl, the Beretta clear and ready, their soft breaths mingling. Her eyes glowed at him in the semidarkness as she whispered, "You turn me on, friend Mack. You really do. But why oh why does it always have to be at a time like this?"

"I'll gladly give you a rain check," he told her. "Did you see the guy?"

"No. I didn't even hear him until—"

"If it was the corporal of the guard, my time's about up. He's going to find a dead soldier at the rear. Are you coming with me or not?"

"I'm not," Smiley quickly replied. She huffed to her feet and gathered the sheaf of papers she'd been inspecting when Bolan arrived. She thrust them at him. "Take these instead. Get them into the right hands. It's very sensitive, so watch who you give them to."

Bolan accepted the papers and secured them inside his shirt. "Who is Chung?" he asked her.

"Around here, they call him the general. I call him Big Daddy, and he eats it up. That should explain my position here. Now you better beat it or you'll blow the whole thing."

"Who's the other guy—the one with all the teeth?"

She tossed her head. "I don't know. He doesn't come very often, and I've never been allowed to meet him."

"What's going on here, Smiley?"

"World War Three, maybe," she replied, smiling tautly.

"You're secure?"

"Sure. I shake my butt, the general will follow me anywhere. Get out of here, Mack. And don't come back. There's nothing here for you. If you must romp, then go find King Fire. That's where it's really at, soldier."

"What is King Fire?"

"A very hush-hush place somewhere near Volcanoes National Park. That's on the big island. Something very curious is going on there. Sounds like your kind of place."

Bolan said, "Last chance, Smiley. I can get you out of here."

"Mack," she replied sadly, "have you any idea how hard I've worked to get *in* here?"

50

He brushed her lips lightly with his own and said, "Live large, lady. Maybe I can at least give you a bonus. The alarms will be sounding pretty soon. You may as well get the points. Count to twenty, then go to the hall and start screaming your head off."

The girl smiled and patted his bottom. He dropped a death medal on the desk and made his exit via the garden door.

"Stay hard," she whispered after him.

Bolan left the sliding door ajar and loped off across the garden. He made it to the shadows at the wall undetected, then waited for the commotion to begin inside the house.

Right on the numbers, it came. Smiley's screams flailed the night. Running feet jarred the ground. Floodlights all around the house erupted with brilliance. A siren began whooping.

And Bolan went over the wall, Beretta at the ready.

The patrol in that sector was caught flat-footed, mouths agape, staring into the brillance of the lights inside the compound.

The Beretta chugged twice in whispering reports that sent a pair of streakers whizzing along the withdrawal route. Both sentries pitched backward without a sound as "old thunder and lightning" put that place behind him. Automatic weapons began chattering from the left flank and a shotgun boomed from the wall, but the reaction was too late. Bolan was already clear —leaving behind, at Kalihi, a hell of a gal who had not, after all, forgotten how to smile.

It was fortunate that he had not come a'blitzing to Kalihi. He knew, however, that he would have to do so, sooner or later. And Smiley Dublin's presence there would greatly complicate the matter.

But then perhaps that was looking too far ahead.

King Fire, maybe, was all the forward look he could handle, at the moment.

King Fire, yeah. It *did* sound like Bolan's kind of place. Certainly that name, whatever it meant, did not have the ring of paradise.

7: Contact

Patterson was at the large wall chart in the tac room when the call came—and he was totally unprepared for it. Later, he would tell a close friend, "I felt like a nervous kid on his first date. It was terrible. My knees went weak and my hands got clammy. I knew I was reacting too much, too heavy—but I just plunged on without giving a damn. The guy just affects you that way. I believe I would have handled a call from the President with more cool. The *nerve* of that fucking guy—I guess that's what got to me."

Mack Bolan had never been above fraternizing with the law—not when it seemed important to do so. It was all in the record—the guy had done it many times before. All the same, the homicide lieutenant who had suddenly become the focus of the worldwide stop-Bolan campaign came very close to missing the contact entirely.

"Get out of here!" he snarled at the cop who brought news of the call.

"Seriously, Lieutenant," the cop insisted. "The guy says he's Mack Bolan. He asked for you by name."

Patterson heaved a disgusted sigh and seized the telephone as though grabbing a miscreant by the nape of the neck. "Yeah, what th' hell is this all about?!" he growled into the instrument.

53

A cool voice replied, "Hellfire in paradise, maybe. Are you Patterson?"

"I am. They tell me you're Mack Bolan. Should I laugh now or later?"

"Better do it now while you can. This is important. Give me a quiz if you'd like, but let's confirm the identity quick."

"Bolan, huh? You're the guy?" Patterson had already decided, deep in his gut, that it *was* Bolan. It was at this point that he lowered his weight to the desk and felt the moisture forming in his palms. "Where'd you get my name, huh?"

"Easy," came the instant reply, the voice warming some. "I simply asked for it. I was told that you're the one who drew the short straw. But I didn't call to wish you luck, Lieutenant. Just observing protocol."

Patterson flashed a desperate glance at another cop in his tac force and made a frantic signal with his free hand, even though he knew that the chances of getting a trace on the call were practically nil. "What do you mean by that?" he asked the nervy bastard at the other end. "What protocol?"

"I have some intelligence to pass along. Figured you'd be the one to handle it intelligently."

"You've got a hell of a goddamned nerve!" Patterson snarled.

"That's my strong point," the guy replied, chuckling. "You've got a weak one. It wears a badge and plays friendly games with a guy called Chung. I guess you've heard of Chung."

"Of course I've heard of Chung!" the lieutenant roared, fuming at himself more so than at the caller. "Don't play cute with me, mister. If you've got something to say, come right out and say it!"

"I've said it. I don't know his name but he's young,

54

tall, skinny, sandy hair worn low on the ears. Drives a new blue Plymouth. Should be easy to identify. You can run him down as the first to report the hit on Angliano. He was ordered to the scene by Oliveras, to check it out. Later he carried the news about Oliveras to Chung. Thought you'd like to know."

"Sure," Patterson snarled. "And we'll take your word for the whole thing, Bolan—sure we will. I'll even—"

"Talk to me intelligently, guy, or I'm hanging up," that voice warned, very icy now.

The lieutenant rubbed a sweating hand on his pants leg and rolled his eyes at the staff of tac cops who'd gathered at his desk. "Hey, I'm sorry," he told the caller. "I lost my cool, I apologize. I appreciate the info. We'll check it out, of course. Look, uh—Bolan? You still there?"

"I'm here."

"We're going to nail you, mister."

"Congratulations. Do you mind if I do a bit of sight-seeing first? It's my first trip to paradise in quite a while."

"You've been here before?"

"Sure, many times. In uniform. I did a few months at Schofield once."

"I guess you know the island pretty well, then."

"Like my back yard at home," the most wanted man in the world replied chattily. "Used to love the big waves up at the north shore."

"You rode the big ones?"

"I enjoyed trying," the guy replied with a chuckle.

"You're still trying the big ones, aren't you?"

"Yeah, I keep trying. What else, Patterson, except to sit down and have a good cry. Crying doesn't get much, does it?"

"I don't cry much, Bolan."

"You don't get much either, Patterson."

The son of a bitch!

The lieutenant cleared his throat and worked diligently at civility. "We do better than a lot of tourist towns."

"Better isn't enough," the cool bastard replied, the voice cold and serious again. "At the moment you're entertaining a whole task force of visiting undesirables. Guys like Odono, Dominick, Flora, Rodani, half a dozen more."

"We know they're here."

"But you don't cry much." The caller chuckled suddenly, heading off a heated retort from the cop. "Okay, I'm out of line. You didn't invent the game—you're just stuck on the rules. I'm not."

"You're going to be. There's no way off this rock for a fugitive, Bolan. We're going to nail you."

"Well, I still think I'll take in a few sights first. You could do the same. Keep an eye on Oliveras. Your cracked badge was given a contract on him."

"You're sure about that?"

"Yeah. In all justice, the guy didn't like the assignment. But my guts say that he took it. Chung doesn't accept negative responses."

The hand that held the phone was shaking again. "Hell, I don't get you, mister!" Patterson growled. "Why should you give a *damn* about Oliveras? You tried him twice yourself. Now you're calling here all worried about his fat hide!"

"No, I didn't try him, Patterson. I've been saving Oliveras. For the same reason that Chung now wants him wasted. Put a good watch on the guy. And get that cracked badge the hell out of the picture. I don't want to start shooting at badges—not even cracked ones."

"Let's set up a meet," Patterson suggested, controlled again. "A white-flag meet. I believe you're a decent guy, deep down. I'd like to help you. Let's meet and talk it over."

The guy laughed at that, but it was a pleasant laugh. "Good try, Patterson. Tell you what. I feel the same about you. Deep down, you're a decent cop just trying to do his job. I'd like to help you, too. So I'll finish my work here as soon as possible, and I'll vacate your Garden of Eden before you have to nail me. Meanwhile you can help me by keeping Oliveras alive. By the way, Lieutenant, do you know who Chung really is?"

Patterson found himself stammering, "He's a—he—I don't know if—"

"He's a genuine general in the Red Chinese army. Why do you suppose an honest-to-God general would be playing muscle games with the mob here in your Garden of Eden?"

"What? What are you—Bolan? Bolan!"

The line was buzzing; the guy was gone.

"Well, can you *believe* that nervy bastard!" Patterson said quietly, as he hung up his own instrument.

"I got it on tape," said one of the tac cops.

Another one laughed nervously as he caught the lieutenant's eye and informed him, "There's a mainland call holding on line four. It's Washington, Justice Department. Guy named Brognola."

"Guy, *hell!*" Patterson snorted, lunging back toward the telephone. "Do you know who Brognola *is?*"

Patterson knew for damned sure, and this was a call he did not have to be persuaded to accept. Harold

Brognola was the number two cop in the country. He was also chief of the federal anti-Bolan forces.

After chatting with the target of it all, however, Brognola came as something of an anticlimax.

"Can you tell me, Mr. Brognola," Lieutenant Patterson asked, right off the bat, "why Mack Bolan should be gunning for a genuine Chinese general? He tells me, just a minute ago, that this genuine general is the Hawaii enforcer for La Cosa Nostra. Now does that make any sense to you?"

"I will be there," Brognola replied curtly, "on the fastest jet I can commandeer."

"Maybe you'd better do that," the HPD lieutenant said with a sigh, just before he hung up on the nation's number two cop. "And you'd better do it damn quick if you want a piece of the action. The guy is on a hellfire tour. He just told me so."

Then the commander of the Honolulu tactical force turned to his crew with a grim face. "General quarters!" he commanded. "Let's get it up. Let's get it *all* up!"

8: From the Woodwork

Bolan located Tommy Anders at one of the luxury hotels along the beach at Waikiki. The comic had a nice two-room suite rigged for light housekeeping, with a balcony overlooking the ocean.

"Hell Jesus, you walk around with more cool than I do," Anders greeted the latest sensation of Oahu. "Do you understand that every cop on this island has been mobilized to look for you? And if that isn't enough, the Oahu Cove has been taken over for the goon squads. They've cancelled the shows through tomorrow and hung out a closed sign. There's more torpedoes in there right now than you'd find at the sub base in Pearl Harbor."

"Yeah," Bolan said, "I just came from there. A guy tried to recruit me. The going price for a hot gun, in case you're interested, is fifty bucks an hour."

Anders smiled and rolled his eyes at that. "Take my advice and hold out for a hundred. What—are they crazy? Guys are actually signing up to die at that price?"

Bolan grinned soberly. "You're forgetting the head money. It's up to about half a mil now."

"It's still a lousy contract. Those recruits should have been standing with me in the lobby when the whitecoats started rolling the stiffs through, a while

59

ago. I counted *ten*, man—ten all in a row." The comic shook his head with the memory of it. "I thought maybe you were bullshitting me. I didn't really expect you to go up there. Why do you do it? For God's sake. How long do you think you can keep this up?"

"Until I die," Bolan replied lightly. He handed over the papers from Chung's office. "Somebody told me to get this into the right hands. I guess you're as right as I can get."

Anders dropped onto a couch and rapidly shuffled through the papers. A moment later he quietly asked, "Where'd you get this stuff?"

"Smiley gave it to me."

The little guy just sat there with a dumb look on his face for a moment, then a smile appeared and spread from ear to ear as he began to chuckle. It was Anders' way of handling heavy emotion; Bolan understood that. The moment passed, and the little guy solemnly declared, "You're a loving Lourdes miracle. Know that? Where is she?"

"She's okay," Bolan assured him. "Full of smiles and mining the mother lode. She's staying put."

"Uh *huh*. Chung, eh?"

"Yeah. Place up near the head of Kalihi Valley. Trans-Pacific Cultural Association."

Anders was frowning now. "I've heard of that. What are they culturing?"

Bolan's gaze snapped to the papers on the couch. "Martial arts, I'd say. That's the inventory."

"Yeah, but . . ." The frown deepened as Anders' attention returned to the intelligence. "Half of this is in Chinese."

"That's the connection," Bolan told him. "Those are training manuals. For military hardware."

"They have this stuff up there? At Kalihi? The hardware, I mean."

Bolan shook his head. "According to Smiley, no. She gave me the same shove you did. Toward Hilo. She called the place King Fire, said it's somewhere in the Volcanoes Park area."

Anders exclaimed, "Oh hell, I have to tell . . ." He rose abruptly from the couch and strode across the room toward a connecting door, then halted at midpoint and pivoted about to give Bolan a solemn smile. "I, uh, didn't mention—I believe you've met my road manager. He's with me permanent now. Mind if I bring him in? This is going to knock you over." He chuckled, adding, "I don't mean literally. Okay if I surprise you?"

Bolan shrugged and returned the smile, but the eyes were wary.

A guy in Bolan's position did not like surprises.

Anders went on to the connecting door and rapped on it lightly.

Bolan went to the balcony and turned his back on the ocean. The moon was holding forth nicely here at leeward, but the balcony was shielded from its direct glow. If he had to be deliberately surprised, he preferred it this way, in semidarkness and with all the available light riding on the object of that surprise.

Anders was speaking into the open doorway to the connecting suite. "Hey, hell, come on in here. It's old home week. Look who I got here."

A tall, athletic young man stepped through that doorway, moving almost as warily as had Bolan. He wore slacks and a rumpled white shirt with a tie pulled down into a loose vee at the throat. He wore, also, a gun harness across the chest.

Bolan's gun hand was hovering at the Beretta when

61

recognition flared. The night had been full of echoes; this one came from beyond Vegas, from almost the very beginning of the Executioner's home-front war. The surprise was Carl Lyons, the L.A. cop who had figured so prominently in Bolan's Southern California campaigns. Later, at Vegas, Bolan had spirited the guy from death's very door.

"It's a hard kick from L.A.," Bolan called gruffly from the balcony.

The cop did a little comic dance and called back, "Get in here, Pointer, before you give the neighborhood a bad name."

The cop and the fugitive, who had shared so much of life and death together, met at the center of the room with a warm four-hand clasp. "Figured it must be you," Lyons said quietly. "Tommy told me about your meeting earlier this evening."

Bolan said, "You're a long way from home turf. You L.A. cops do get around."

"I'm on indefinite leave," Lyons explained. His gaze flicked to the smiling Anders. "Managing the hottest comic in the land."

"With gunleather," Bolan observed, smiling.

"Yeah," Anders put in drily. "Actually, I believe the guy is under orders to shoot me first time I bomb."

Lyons said, "I'd have shot you a hundred times by now."

"Aw, come on," the comic protested. His face fell suddenly into sober lines as he updated his partner to the latest news. "Mack located Smiley. She's infiltrated the Chung organization and doing great."

An expression of relief spread over the cop's face. He lit a cigarette to cover the emotion, then squeezed Bolan's arm and stepped into a small service kitchen.

"Coffee, anyone?" he asked lightly. "Sit down. I'll serve."

Bolan removed his jacket and draped it over the back of a chair, then sat down across the table from Anders. He was watching Lyons as he quietly inquired of the comic, "You said permanent—you're a team, now?"

"Yeah. My boss signs his paychecks. Please don't ask any more."

Bolan nodded and lit a cigarette. Lyons came over balancing three cups and carrying an electric percolator.

"You told me there was nothing in the woodwork," Bolan pointedly reminded Anders.

"Carl isn't in the woodwork," Anders replied, his face blankly innocent. "He's right out in the open, with me."

"How many more are not in the woodwork?" Bolan asked lightly.

Lyons chuckled and shoved coffee at him, then took a chair between the two. "It's a pretty heavy operation, Mack," he explained.

"Smiley used the word *sensitive*," Bolan said.

"Okay, that's a good one."

Bolan tasted the coffee and took a long pull at the cigarette. A heavy, almost embarrassed silence ruled that table for a moment. Bolan sent the cigarette smoke spiraling toward the ceiling and said, "Then it's no time for cozy games. You'd better level with me."

"Wish we could," Lyons muttered.

"Show him the intelligence, Anders."

The comic said, "Oh. Yeah."

Moments later, Lyons was lighting his second cigarette while directing a troubled gaze at the pile of

63

papers. "Okay, so you're onto it," he commented heavily to Bolan. "Where'd you get this?"

"Smiley passed it to me."

"I see."

"I don't," Bolan said.

Lyons and Anders exchanged uncomfortable glances.

"We can't discuss this, Mack," Anders said, very softly.

Bolan replied, just as softly, "Bull." He stood up, put on his jacket, said, "Stay clear," and headed for the door.

Lyons protested, "Hey, dammit!"

Bolan had the door open. He turned back with a sober smile. "It's okay,"² he said, and went out the door.

He was halfway to the elevator when a door opened behind him and a commanding female voice called out, "Okay, Captain Hard! Your way, then. To the rear march, and doubledamnquick!"

Bolan came around grinning.

He was beyond surprise on this night of echoes.

And Toby Ranger, brass mouth and all hundred pounds of bristling womanhood, looked good enough to die for.

The game in Hawaii had abruptly taken on an entirely new dimension.

9: Sogging It

There were no embraces this time, nor was there any casual camaraderie or light humor. This was a business meeting, in the strictest sense. And it was quite evident that Toby Ranger was the outranker here.

The meeting was held in the suite that connected to Anders'. This was, obviously, the working suite. Tools of the trade were scattered about everywhere— road maps, aeronautical charts, tourist brochures of the various islands, an imposing rogue's gallery of glossy mug shots, weapons, graphs, official papers.

A sectional aero chart of the island of Hawaii bore the tracks of an exhaustive search operation.

Tommy Anders occupied a chair near the connecting door. Lyons was at the small bar that separated the cooking and dining areas. Toby Ranger, sheer golden dynamite in bare legs, skimpy shorts, and a clinging, no-bra knit top, was posed at the balcony doorway, in half-profile and staring gloomily into the night.

At the table, Bolan completed an examination of the search chart and tiredly commented, "Looks like you've covered it all. And you found nothing at all?"

"Not a damn thing," Toby sniffed, without breaking the pose.

"It's been strictly an air search?"

"Yes. Understand—that's rough country. It goes from sea level to nearly fourteen thousand feet without even thinking about it. It's mountains, cliffs, canyons, meandering valleys, forests, lava flows, craters—and I mean craters, very active ones. And it's a damn big island."

"How many are you?" Bolan quietly asked.

"You've got it right here," Toby replied.

"Plus, of course, Smiley," Anders put in soberly.

"Do you have a detail map of the national park area?"

Toby stepped over to the table, did some shuffling, and came up with a geodetic survey map. "This is about the closest thing to it," she said, opening the map and leaning over Bolan's shoulder to study it with him.

He had a tough time concentrating on the problem. Toby Ranger had shared with him an exotic stage of the human experience such as those other friends present here were biologically unable to do.

Bolan growled, "Toby, get the hell off my body."

She did so, but slowly, sliding along his arm to a chair close alongside. "There are no green pastures on that map, soldier," she said coolly—adding, under her breath, "Dammit."

The two of them *had* found a brief stretch of "green pasture"—a damned brief one, along the withdrawal route from Detroit—and much too recently to easily forget. Bolan had fallen a bit in love with the brass-pantied fed, and there had been idyllic moments in the wake of that horror with the unlucky Georgette Chableu, the deceased member of the Ranger Girls. Actually, he admitted to himself, Bolan had been a bit in love with each of those girls. But there was no

66

room for romance in the hellfire existence of a living dead man. Bolan knew that and accepted it. Toby knew it, also. Green pastures, no.

Bolan told the the lady, "Plenty of fire there, though."

"Yes," she murmured, "those volcanoes still rumble and boil. During my last overflight, I saw several huge glowing fissures." She tapped the chart with a finger. "Right about here."

"You know the legend of Pele?" he asked absently.

"She's the fire goddess, isn't she?"

"Yeah. According to the legend, she lives in Kilauea Crater. She dances in the lava fountains of Halemaumau Firepit, giving birth to the island in the constant outpouring of molten rock. The island actually is growing continually."

"That's very interesting," Toby commented. "But hardly to the point."

"Maybe it is," Bolan said thoughtfully. "King Fire could be entirely symbolic. Or it could be descriptive of a location. And we know—or we think we know—that it's somewhere around the volcanoes."

"That isn't quite good enough," Toby said. "It would take incredible luck plus a battalion of ground searchers to find the place—going on what we know or think we know."

Bolan had to admit the truth of that.

He'd spent time on that island, and he knew what the terrain was like over there.

"There's only one way to go, then," Bolan announced somberly.

"What way is that?"

"My way," he replied.

"Thunder and lightning," Lyons observed, from the sideline.

67

"That's the way."

"Mother Pele, move over," Anders commented in a worried voice.

Lyons sighed and said, "No good, Mack. It's a direct violation of our charter. Our job is to *not*—"

"Carl!" the girl cautioned him.

"Bullshit, Toby," Lyons argued. "Look—all of us have drunk blood with this guy. He's saved all our butts, each of us at one time or another—for some of us, more than once. Now either we go or we don't go—but I damned sure can't stomach any more of this mincing around at the edge. I'm sure as hell not going to *use* the guy!"

"That's not fair!" Toby flared back. "I've had no such intention!"

Bolan had suddenly become a third person. He lit a cigarette and went to the balcony. It seemed that a crisis in government was brewing in that hotel suite; he wanted no part of it. He closed the door and sat on the railing, smoking and trying to ignore the rise of heated voices inside.

Presently the door opened and Toby softly called, "Mack . . ."

He stepped inside, went to his jacket, put it on. "I work better alone, anyway," he said quietly. "Just stay out of my way, all of you. I want no friendly blood on my hands."

"Wait a minute, dammit!" Lyons said miserably.

"We voted to put it on the table," Anders explained.

The Bolan gaze fell on Toby Ranger. "Was it unanimous?"

Her eyes fell and she replied, "Yes. We want you to know the setup. Our data bank in Washington is labeled SOG-3. That means that we are Unit Three of the Sensitive Operations Group. I can't give you

68

the chain of command, except to say that we operate indirectly from the office of the United States Marshal."

"Brognola your boss?"

"Possibly. We've met. But we have no direct line to him."

Lyons explained, "We sort of, uh, float free—you know. The paychecks and expense vouchers are washed enroute to us. The key word in our charter is 'sensitive.' We walk the borderlines between law and disorder."

"The hellgrounds," Bolan interpreted it, smiling soberly.

"Hellgrounds, right," Lyons agreed, still somewhat embarrassed by the whole charade. "I guess someone took a leaf from your notebook. They pulled us together shortly after the blast at Vegas. Said we'd worked good as a team there. Gave us a charter, a map to hell, and a gentle shove in the general direction. Toby and Smiley, Tommy and myself—we're Unit Three. Georgette Chableu and Sally Palmer drew another unit. The entire SOG operation is, uh—well, I said it. Someone took a leaf from your book."

"Brognola," Bolan said, smiling.

"Who knows? Maybe so."

Bolan knew. It was the same portfolio offered him by Brognola in Miami, too many eternities ago. Bolan had turned it down. Apparently the idea had proven too strong for Brognola to drop it entirely.

Toby was saying, "We do have one advantage that you do not. We can request direct support from any law enforcement agency in the country. And we can use their facilities."

Anders added, "Emergencies only, of course."

69

"The idea," Lyons said, "is to remain in the wood-work to the greatest degree possible."

Toby murmured, "So you can see why we—even with you—I mean, why we couldn't . . ."

Bolan said, "Forget it." He pinned the girl with a penetrating gaze. "You weren't Sogging it in Detroit?"

She shook her head. "It was just as I told you at the time. I just didn't give you all of it. Georgette's unit had been working a Canadian connection. The head office let me look for her because—because we had been very close. I was operating independently in Detroit, just as I told you."

Bolan smiled soberly, remembering. "You didn't go back? After . . . ?"

"No. Brave words notwithstanding, I did not. I re-joined the unit. We've been on this case ever since."

Lyons said, "Smiley was our advance girl. She followed Lou Topacetti here from Chicago and made the initial infiltration. We didn't really know exactly what we were looking for, at the moment. Just following the drift."

"And the drift was westward," Bolan commented.

"Yeah. From all the 'sheds. Boston, New York—name the family, it was sending headpower. You get curious about movements like that."

Bolan nodded. He understood perfectly. The same movements had brought the Executioner to Hawaii.

Toby said, "When Smiley dropped from sight, I started getting visions of Detroit."

Bolan could sympathize with that, also. It had been his first vision.

"We got Tommy booked into the Cove. That wasn't hard to do. He worked that angle while Carl and I beat the bushes of these islands."

70

"And," Lyons added, scowling, "the morgues and beaches."

Toby continued: "Two weeks ago we began to accept the idea that we'd probably never see Smiley again. It was about that same time when we began getting a glimmer of the full scope of the power behind Chung. He's a real mystery man. And he really has—"

"It's a strange deal," Lyons interrupted. "This guy Chung popped up from nowhere a little less than a year ago and started taking over these islands. There seems to be a Hong Kong connection, but that's not certain. Mystery man, yeah. Every cop in the area has heard the name but none has seen the face. FBI wiretaps began picking up the name in all of the mainland strongholds and we got a report straight out of the *commissione* that a Chinese enforcer had been chartered for the islands state. Nobody knows who he really is or anything about the guy—except that his presence here is suffocating the place."

"Smiley knows," Bolan said quietly.

"Well, sure—*now*. But—"

"He's General Loon Chuk Wan, People's Republic of China."

Silence ruled that room for a long moment. Toby paced over to the balcony door to again consult the night skies. Lyons lit a cigarette. Anders broke the silence.

"That's some hell of an ethnic joke," the comic quietly declared.

"No joke at all," Bolan murmured.

"Do the old men back home know it?" asked Lyons.

"Probably," Bolan mused. "Why else the sudden link-up?"

"Doesn't fit, that's why," Lyons said. "The mob

71

boys are notorious flag wavers. Strongly anti-communist. I can't see a conscious link-up there."

"You don't give the old men enough credit," Bolan argued. "They have more practical vision than many of our statesmen. I've been smelling this dog ever since San Francisco. Accords are coming, detente is in the wind. The old men, whatever else they may be, can never be accused of sleeping when opportunity comes scratching at the door. They're getting their shots in first. And Chung is obviously one of those shots."

"But what's in it for Chung or Loon or whatever?" Toby wondered.

"There's the rub," said Bolan.

Anders corrected that. "There's the SOG. It's exactly what we've been looking for, isn't it?"

"Guess it is," Lyons quietly agreed. "Ever since Vegas."

Toby snatched a cigarette from the table, lit it with a flair, and began prancing back and forth with considerable agitation.

Bolan suggested, "Cool it. It's a very simple problem."

"Simple *hell!*" she fumed. "For you, maybe, Captain Blitz. But not for the rest of the world. We could be sitting atop World War Three here, the powder keg anyway."

"Smiley said almost the exact thing," Bolan mused. "But I don't buy it. I would have to guess that Chung is a dissident. He's playing some game on his own— or, at least, for the benefit of some disfavored faction back home. I see the problem as a simple smoke-out. Expose the guy. Bust his operation. His government will abandon him. They'd string him up, probably, if he ever returned home."

72

"Sounds like a SOG mission to me," Anders said gloomily.

"They're stockpiling arms somewhere around here," Bolan pointed out. "Some damned exotic arms. I know what the mob hopes to buy from that. *The Big Thing.* The question mark is Chung. What does he hope to buy? Official tensions between the nations? A loss of face that would be certain to wreck the slow march to detente? Or is he simply a bandit who's decided it's better to be rich than red?"

"That is precisely what I mean!" Toby said. "It's very complex—not simple at all. I want a conference with the front office."

Bolan said calmly, "You know better, Toby. Those people upstairs will be stumbling around for months trying to arrive at some great diplomatic moment. By the time that show got moving, this one could be long gone—dispersed anywhere in the wide world. You think Hawaii is a big island? Try finding King Fire somewhere on Island Earth."

"Mack's right," Lyons decided. "If we contact the front now, their first order of business will be to clamp a freeze on everything."

"That's probably true," Toby agreed, gnawing at a delectable lower lip.

"Meanwhile," Bolan said quietly, "our girl Smiley is in a very bad position. It's unnecessary, now. I should have brought her out—kicking and screaming, if necessary, but out."

"Let's SOG it," suggested Anders.

"Agreed," Lyons said, tight-lipped.

"Dammit," said Toby Ranger.

"Mack's way," Anders voted.

"Agreed," Lyons seconded.

"Dammit!" complained the outranker.

6   73

"We can't find King Fire," Bolan explained. "So we'll have to bring King Fire to us. We hit Kalihi. At dawn."

"Dammit, just dammit!" Toby yelled.

"That makes it unanimous," said the Executioner. He turned to Carl Lyons with a grim smile. "Think you could scare up a hang glider on short notice?"

"A what? You mean those manned kite gadgets?"

Bolan's gaze was seeking the moonlit sky outside. "Yeah. I've never tried it in this particular area, but— why not? We have the currents, we have the heights. Why not?"

"What are you talking about?" Toby demanded worriedly.

Very soberly, Bolan told her, "I'm talking about dropping in on the general like a big bird."

"A big fire bird," Anders said, awed by the thought.

"A thunder bird," Toby sarcastically corrected Anders. "Captain Thunder, honey, you have got to be out of your loving mind!"

"So what's new?" Bolan asked quietly. "We hit at dawn."

The game had definitely changed.

The Executioner had taken on allies.

10: Soaring

Hang gliding could be a tricky business, even for an expert. Bolan was no expert, but he was not exactly a novice either. He had tried the big kites on several occasions during the pre-war, but always along coastal areas where the wind was predictable and the updrafts certain.

Once he had sustained a fifteen-mile flight along the Southern California coast—then again, once he'd gone down like a rock to within a few feet of the beach, catching enough lift at the last moment to send him hurtling out into the water instead of smashing to certain death on the rocks.

There was no saving water waiting at the bottom of this try.

The valley floor lay several thousand feet below. Between Bolan and his target were plunging slopes and wild forests, rocky gorges, hazards of every type known to gliding. Worse yet, the wind patterns were tricky, unpredictable. Severe downdrafts on the lee-ward side of the mountains were a distinct possibility —even "dead fall" or "swirl" areas could be awaiting the venturer.

Natural hazards were not, of course, the entire problem. Bolan realized that he had no direct control over the human events that might await him at the end of the journey. He could set up the scene, put the actors in motion, and hope that everyone reacted properly to the cues of the moment. Once airborne, however, he would be pretty much at the mercy of all the variables that could enter the situation.

With all that, Bolan still considered it a sound plan.

Toby, of course, did not. She had denounced it bitterly, washed her hands of it, then—as Bolan had known she would—actively entered into the tactical planning and added some positive touches of her own.

Bolan had great respect for the plucky lady, and with good cause. She had a mind of her own, naturally —and he granted her that. She also had the guts of any man, and he loved her for that.

As for the bickering and the brass mouth, most of it was her way of letting off steam, equalizing tensions; Bolan understood that, also.

Lyons had found no difficulty obtaining the glider. Soaring was becoming a popular sport in the islands. There were several glider clubs in the Honolulu district. He even brought back a tipsheet on the wind and terrain characteristics for the preferred soaring areas on Oahu. Unhappily, though, the leeward side of the Koolau Mountains enjoyed very little prestige as a soaring area for hang gliders. None, in fact, at all.

The glider itself was not the sort of thing to inspire confidence in the novice. Bolan remembered his own hesitation to entrust his life to the flimsy contraption that first time out. The thing was no more than a light aluminum framework supporting a few yards of nylon, a hang bar, and seat harness. Lyons had come closer to a proper description of the contraption when he referred to it as a kite. "Hang gliding" was more definitive of the actual operation. You simply grabbed the bar, hung on, and leaped off a cliff. That took care of raw courage. The rest was in the hands of friendly air currents, great physical instincts, and an understanding of the principles of flight.

It could be an exhilarating experience. With good currents, a guy could soar like an albatross for hours—and even *feel* like one. In good soaring areas, it was usually the skill of the pilot rather than any other condition that dictated the length of flight. Theoretically, a guy could fly for as long as he could hang there and control the thing.

And now Bolan was alone in the Koolau Mountains and ready for his moment of truth. The glider was assembled and ready, situation *go* with the wind strong and steady.

He was poised atop a high peak with a sheer drop and a clear view to both windward and leeward—a position where the currents were definitely updrafting as they lifted above the mountain range.

He was equipped for hard combat. The impressive .44 AutoMag was strapped to his hip, complementing the shoulder-rigged Beretta. Grenades, smokers, and incendiaries dangled from chest and waist belts. He wore goggles and a throat mike/earphone rig, the latter connected to a small CB transceiver at his waist.

He took a final sampling of the currents, studied his chronometer, then pressed the mike switch and requested, "Signal check."

Lyons' voice bounced back immediately from the line position on the valley floor. "Five square. A-OK here."

"Same. Ready for launch. Stand by."

The ocean horizon to windward was glowing redly with the hint of direct sunlight. The moon was down. To windward, the terrain was clearly visible in the gray

77

dawn. The leeward side and particularly Kalihi had not yet been touched by daybreak. It would be, very soon now. Bolan had contemplated a five-minute flight. The timing was vitally important; thus, his ability to maneuver and navigate the proper course was the key to success.

He watched the eastern horizon and lofted the big kite into position overhead, awaiting the launch moment. The wind was a living force now, tugging at the nylon, puffing and popping it, a sudden gust nearly lifting Bolan off his feet.

Then the moment arrived.

He took three running steps and leaped into the bosom of his brother, the wind.

For a breathless second his brother did not seem to know that he was there, or did not care. Man and kite dropped straight down for perhaps twenty feet, then suddenly he was soaring off into a wide turn and climbing, riding the updraft from windward, rising high above the launch point and angling leeward.

Even more dramatic than the fall was the rise. In a twinkling, it seemed, he was several hundred feet above the highest terrain and still climbing. The entire island seemed to lay out to his view—and, yeah, he knew how an eagle felt.

Bolan cinched himself into the harness and activated his throat mike. "Okay, I'm airborne," he reported to the ground troops.

The relieved voice of Carl Lyons responded. "Where away?"

"On course and soaring. Begin your move at the mark . . . stand by . . . *mark*."

"Roger. Moving."

So much for timing.

The rest was in the hands of the variables.

78

And perhaps Toby Ranger had been right, after all. Maybe it was a nutty plan.

He'd penetrated the joint at ground level once before; certainly he could have done so again. The defenses would certainly be heavily bolstered now, however. And penetration was not the only name of the game.

He meant to get Smiley Dublin out of there—whole body. That could take some argument; like Toby, Smiley had a mind of her own. That was the only thing that made these people effective in the toughest business going.

He meant also to jar the hell out of Chung's self-confidence. The idea was to go in soft and come out hard—damned hard, blitzing hard. He wanted to get the Chinaman running scared—all the way to King Fire.

Jonathan Livingston Thunderbird just possibly might attain all mission goals.

But, yeah—it was now all in the hands of Bolan's brother, the universe.

Hang in there, he thought he heard his brother say.

And Bolan replied, "Sure. What else?"

11: The Bolan Effect

The night had been hard on Smiley Dublin, since Mack Bolan's sneak visit. The general had stormed around in a rage for most of an hour, tongue-lashing the security forces and personally overseeing the placement of stronger defenses. Then had come the grim march of visitors for the roundtable conferences and strategy sessions.

Lou Topacetti came with a contingent of hardfaced Occidentals, then Pensa and Rodani arrived with a mixed and motley bag from the Oahu Cove. Pete Dominick and Marty Flora, the New York reps, came in an hour or so after the others—via helicopter and obviously from some place afar; they were traveling light, bringing only their personal triggermen.

Smiley herself was not in bad graces. She was, to her delight, the heroine of the night. The general even allowed her to fuss around in the role of hostess, seeing to the comfort and refreshment of the guests. She was not, of course, privy to the secrets of the council chamber, but her occasional presence in there was tolerated and even furtively appreciated by some of the visitors who seemed to find it difficult to keep their eyes off her.

There was more to spying than actual eavesdropping on secret discussions. Much could be gathered by the mental atmosphere in a room, by attitudes between participants, by mere identification of those present— sometimes by the placement of a lifted eyebrow or the difference between a smile and a smirk.

Smiley Dublin knew her business, and she was a working girl. She worked for everything she got and what she got was usually reliable.

The conference began winding down at about four o'clock when Dominick and Flora bustled back to their helicopter and took off. The house and grounds continued to be cluttered with wandering groups of nervous men until about five, when Pensa and Rodani departed with their contingent. Only Topacetti and his group of professional guns stayed on, Lou himself remaining behind closed doors with Chung, the torpedoes taking station somewhere outside.

Smiley had been "Topacetti's broad" at the beginning of the Hawaii stand. The general had noticed her one evening and had expressed an interest in her, whereupon Lou the Screw grandly handed her over on a silver platter. Topacetti had not given her so much as a direct gaze since. By a normal girl in a normal situation, such treatment could be regarded as the ultimate indignity. To Smiley Dublin, wise in the ways of jungle protocol, it was only proper reward for a hard-working gal who knew the way to a man's heart as well as to his ambitions.

"Treat the Chinaman right," Lou had advised her. "He's going to be a very big man some day. That couldn't hurt neither of us, if you know what I mean."

Smiley had known full well what Topacetti meant. She knew, also, how to "treat the Chinaman right."

Smiley Dublin was a line-of-duty whore, sure, and she was a gal who worked at her job. The thought bothered her not a whit. She did not feel "dirtied" by that kind of sex. Nor did she feel morally uplifted via any manner of reverse reasoning which could have viewed line-of-duty sex as some special sacrifice. It was a weapon, a tool of the trade—period—and a hell of an effective tool. A male operative could not have become so close to General Chung so quickly—perhaps not at all.

The general was apparently thoroughly infatuated with his American beauty. He treated her very well, with tenderness and respect—and there had been some genuinely touching moments between them. Smiley was a realistic pro, though. She never lost sight of who, why, and where she was; it was a job; Chung was the enemy. All else was fantasy. She had learned just enough about Chung and his operation to realize that he was a very dangerous man, that his operation posed a direct threat to the nation.

The dramatic appearance of Mack Bolan upon the scene was the most reassuring event of the stand. Smiley knew him to be a tremendously effective instrument of change. She had been present in Las Vegas when he worked his magic there, so she knew the man's effect from a firsthand point of view. Also, Smiley had been walking the same dark landscapes as Bolan ever since—and she knew his effect from the enemy viewpoint. Even so, it seemed remarkable to her that this lone man, working totally without official sanctions, could create such chaos in the enemy ranks simply by appearing in their midst and killing a few of them.

These were tough, tough men.

It did not seem rational that they should react with such panic to the threat of *any* one man. Still, Smiley had seen the phenomenon time and again. When Bolan showed up, the pack howled and scampered.

She had been surreptitiously studying these men

during the long night in an effort to understand this effect. Fear was a natural human emotion, certainly; even very tough people knew the meaning of fear. But fear itself was but a simple ingredient of the overall brew that was the Bolan Effect, a mere constituent of the all-pervading force that enveloped these brawling bruisers—that seeped into their guts and minds, and converted them to weeping willies and nail-biting nellies.

It was, yes, phenomenal.

The general himself had been greatly shaken by the event. He had been transformed in a twinkling from an imperious and smug potentate into an anxious, uncertain mortal seeking reassurance and support from those he had come to dominate.

The Bolan Effect, yes. Smiley knew that it was there. She had noted it, studied it. Still she could not fully understand it. Nor, she imagined, did these others. They simply got together and talked themselves back up.

The strategy seemed to work. The general appeared tired and drawn at the end of that night, but he was firmly back in the saddle again. Topacetti's torpedoes were remaining aboard to bolster the defenses of the stronghold, and apparently Lou the Screw was remaining, also. The general and his man Friday emerged from the conference room at just a few minutes before dawn, arm in arm and tiredly chuckling over some secret joke. As the men stepped into the corridor, Smiley had overheard Topacetti mutter, "He'd just better *not* try King Fire." A joke, sure—or a deep fear expressed openly in laughing terms.

But Chung was his old self. He allowed Smiley to send a menu to the kitchen, "for breakfast, just for the three of us," and decided to take it on the garden patio.

"Perhaps you should get a wrap, my dear," he suggested to Smiley. "Lotus blossoms are prone to shiver in the morning dew."

It was a veiled rebuke for her habit of taking early-morning, near-nude strolls in the garden, a practice which had caused Chung mild distress. He had never made an issue of the thing except for passing comments to the effect that it was "not good for the men." On this particular morning, Smiley was better covered than usual. Still, the sheer pajamas did tend to cling at strategic points.

She yielded to the general's sensitivities this time, telling him, "You're right, thanks. I'll meet you outside."

Smiley went up to her room and pulled on a sheer kimono, studied the effect in her mirror, smiled, and went down to join the general and his guest for breakfast.

There was something to be said for the Dublin Effect, as well.

Two pistol-packing orderlies were lighting the Oriental lanterns on the patio when she stepped outside. One of them smiled at her and went to turn off the floodlights. Armed men wandered everywhere out there. Chung and Topacetti were strolling aimlessly nearby, heads bent, silent. The sky was turning gray and the feeling of daybreak was in the air.

Smiley went over to the table and began pouring coffee from the silver service that had just been brought out. Chung had noted her appearance and was steering Lou the Screw toward the table when Captain Wu, the security chief, came around the corner on a jog trot from the front of the house.

"An American lady is at the gate," Wu reported to the general. "She says that her car has broken. The lady requests to use the telephone that she may receive assistance."

Smiley had ceased smiling over the stilted English of the Hong Kong commandos. The general would not allow use of the native tongue in his presence. "We forge new habits through constant practice," he had once admonished a follower.

He was now giving his security chief a hard look as he replied to the report. "This is not a monumental decision, Captain. Surely you could handle it on your own."

"The lady's car is poised at our drive, General," Wu explained. "It is my thought that it may prove to our comfort if our own mechanic might assist the lady."

"I leave that to your discretion, Captain," Chung replied brusquely and continued on along the garden path toward Smiley.

The captain spun away and disappeared around the corner of the house.

Before Chung had taken two good paces, an alarmed American voice screamed from the gate area, *"Lady! Lady!—your car's rolling!"*

Another man yelled something in Chinese—a command of some sort.

Chung and Topacetti halted and turned toward the scene of disturbance.

A light machine gun began chattering, then another quickly joined in.

A deafening roar immediately eclipsed all other sounds of the morning as a bright flash enveloped the forward wall area.

The general and his guest dived to the ground while other men raced toward the explosion.

It had all come so quickly, with such thunderous precision, this transition from peace to war. And Smiley Dublin did not have to ponder the effect; she recognized it.

She whirled away from the table and ran into the garden, dodging through the suddenly erupting field of running men, just in time to directly experience the *pièce de résistance*.

Chung had risen to one knee and appeared to be rooted there. Topacetti was kneeling beside him, a pistol in his hand, waving it in the general direction of the front grounds and screaming something at the men who ran past him.

Smiley's attention was diverted to the opposite direction. Something had registered in a corner of her vision; she had become aware of an object like a shadow in the sky, moving swiftly and silently about fifty feet above the south wall, descending rapidly and swooping into the stronghold.

Her first incredulous thought concerned the size of that huge bird, but even before her intellect had time to reject that assumption, the thing was close enough to identify and she could only marvel at the audacity of that unbelievable man who was attacking a walled fortress from the belly of a kite.

Someone in the garden area screamed a warning.

Both Chung and Topacetti whirled around to confront the thing that was now skimming across the lotus pond at almost ground level. Lou the Screw began firing at it. A single clap of thunder issued from the kite as a pencil-flame leapt out. Smiley saw Topacetti pitch over onto his back as the general scrambled toward the house.

Then suddenly the thing was down and the general was down beneath it. A series of quaking explosions

86

were now rocking the stronghold in all sectors. Men were yelling and running in all directions like frantic ants.

Smiley was surprised to find herself running, also, for God knew what reason. She took cover at the patio wall and tried to gather herself together, to assess the situation and find her place in it.

It had been such a stunning, jolting departure from reality into a nightmarish fantasy of hell unleashed. Flames were now leaping from the roof of the house. Dense smoke was billowing up from various points about the grounds. The explosions continued and gunfire was everywhere.

The Bolan Effect, yes. It was no fantasy. It was a reality which none could rationalize into their own fantasies. Smiley thought she understood it now.

A tall figure in black ran past her as a familiar voice coolly commanded, "Stay put, Smiley!"

The girl did as she was told. Hell itself was assaulting the stronghold. And Smiley herself was frozen in the grip of the Bolan Effect.

And, yes, she understood it now. It was much more than mere fear. It was an instinctive recognition of doomsday on the march. And the very soul trembled in that awareness.

12: Trail Blazing

Chung's stronghold was nestled in a semi-box canyon set into the western slope of the mountain, with high ground to the south and east, undulating terrain rolling out west and north. The building was a rectangular structure aligned north-south, with the main entrance at the north side.

Gardens flanked east and west, the west side being the primary center of outdoor activity with its lotus pond, fountains, and patios. The only gate was set into the northwest corner of the wall, about a hundred feet by a circling inner drive from the parking area at the north end.

Bolan's flight plan called for a reconnaissance pass from north to south at relatively high altitude, then a play-by-ear descent keyed to the numbers of the diversion plan and as dictated by the realities of the soaring situation.

The initial approach had gone drawing-board perfect, straight on the numbers. Soaring at an altitude of roughly two hundred feet, he skirted the east side of the box in an eagle recon, immediately spotting Toby's vehicle, which was halted atop the slope about fifty feet above the gate.

The floodlights in the west garden had just been extinguished. The landscape in the target zone was receiving the first soft touch of daybreak while, behind Bolan, the western slope of the mountain loomed darkly to provide the closest thing to invisibility his flight was likely to find.

He dropped fifty feet in the south turn and made a reverse-course run directly above the house.

During that pass, Toby came into view walking slowly up the slope toward her vehicle and, at that same instant, the quartz chronometer on Bolan's wrist beeped faintly, signaling the beginning of the final countdown.

Yeah, right on the numbers.

He went into a wide, climbing turn at the north boundary and touched his mike button for the final check. "Situation," he requested.

"We have a go," Lyons immediately replied.

"Commencing bomb run," Bolan reported as he banked into the north-south low-level run.

Off to his right, Toby Ranger was now sprinting for cover and Lyons was rolling from the vehicle into the vegetation lining the drive, the car moving freely along toward the gate. A muffled voice directly below shouted something and machine-gun fire split the calm.

It was an alert defense—but not, Bolan hoped, alert enough.

As he swooped above the house on his final pass, he was offloading munitions—HE frags, burners, smokers—in a calculated pattern keyed to time-delay fuses.

Toby's vehicle with its impact charge hit the front wall and sent shock waves which even Bolan experienced as he executed the turn onto final approach. The towering fireball set the stage for Bolan's entrance, with apparently everybody on those hellgrounds down there racing toward the far side of the stronghold.

He dropped another fifty feet as he skimmed over the south wall and swooped in, AutoMag at the ready.

People were in motion everywhere and there were sounds of a firefight outside the walls to the west. By now, also, the time fuses were beginning to detonate the aerial drops, and Bolan was descending into absolute pandemonium.

Like a gift from heaven, the bristly head of the Chinese general came into view less than twenty yards downwind. Bolan leaned into the course correction to line up on the guy as someone off to starboard screamed a warning and took a wild shot at him.

Chung and a pistol-waving companion whirled into the confrontation. In that split second, Bolan vaguely recognized the guy with the pistol which was now unloading on him in wild rapidfire. The .44 roared with a mind of its own and the guy with the pistol went down. Chung, apparently unarmed, was trying to scrambled clear of certain collision with the winged invader, but Bolan rode him to ground, slipping clear of the harness at the moment of impact and smartly addressing that bristly head with the butt of the Auto-Mag.

Chung went limp as the glider settled over him. Bolan danced clear and whirled into an attack by two Orientals who were running at him from the patio. A flash-vision of Smiley Dublin sprinting across the background stayed his response for a heartbeat; their guns were quicker, but his was surer. A pair of thunderous retorts from the blazing .44 sent the two hurtling off at diverging angles as Bolan moved on between them and toward the house.

Smiley had flung herself to the ground behind a low wall at the patio. Bolan issued a terse command as

90

he ran past her position to scatter incendiaries into the ground-level interior.

He collected her on the return trip and pulled her through lung-biting chemical smoke to where he'd left General Chung-Loon.

"Wh-what're we doing?" the girl gasped as Bolan roughly hauled Chung to his feet.

The general was conscious, feebly so—dazed but aware.

"It's bust-out time," Bolan snapped. "On the numbers and hurry-hurry." He shoved Chung forward and warned, "You too, General. Move it quick or stop moving forever."

Chung understood that message. He jerked himself upright and muttered, "As you wish."

They moved unmolested through the pandemonium and to the vehicle area at the front of the house. There was no more gunfire in this sector. A vehicle was burning and flames were also whooshing from the front door of the house.

Bolan selected a convertible with the keys lying atop the dashboard. "Perfect," he said. He pushed Smiley into the driver's seat and told her, "Put the top down and get ready for a stately exit."

The girl seemed almost as dazed as Chung, but her reflexes were functioning well enough. She started the engine and worked the roof mechanism while Bolan gave final words to his hostage.

"Behave yourself," he told the guy, "and you could live through this yet."

The general had no argument left in him.

He meekly climbed into the back seat at Bolan's bidding and sat himself down on the rear deck above the seat, parade fashion—but there would be no confetti for this ride.

Bolan took position below the general, the muzzle of the big .44 in clear view at the guy's face, and he instructed Smiley, "Okay, slow and easy, out we go. Let's hear some horn."

They left in that fashion, the convertible, with horn blaring, moving slowly along the drive and through the shattered gate, the general seated stiffly up top with a gun at his mouth, excited commands in the Chinese language from the sidelines punctuating the stunned drama of that daring withdrawal.

Bolan could see agitated men moving about quietly in the smoke along that drive as Smiley maneuvered to avoid the wrecked vehicle at the gate, but none challenged the trump hand which he held.

Looking back from the knoll which Toby Ranger's stalled vehicle had occupied a scant few minutes earlier, the scene back there was one for Bolan's book. The house was an inferno, with roiling flames surging high above the pall of smoke that overhung the entire stronghold. The wall near the gate was demolished, and that entire sector was pockmarked with line patterns of bullet holes. Lifeless bodies were strewn around back there and more lay along the withdrawal route, even to the knoll.

Bolan halted the car at that point, in clear view of those below, to shove his hostage to the ground, telling him, "Okay, guy, you lucked it this time. If you're smart, you'll beat it home now and forget you ever heard of King Fire."

The general's eyes quivered at that, but he said nothing except, "The lady. You will release her, also?"

"Not here," Bolan replied in the ice voice. "I want no pursuit, Chung. Get down there and see to that."

Chung shot his lady a helpless look and lurched off down the drive.

92

Quietly, Bolan commanded, "Go, Smiley."

"I almost feel sorry for him," she murmured as she put the car in motion.

"I sometimes feel sorry for rattlesnakes, too," Bolan told her. "Stop just around this next curve. We have troops to embark."

She pulled over where directed. Toby Ranger and Carl Lyons stepped out of the growth at the side of the road, automatic weapons cradled casually at their chests, and climbed aboard.

Smiley began to weep.

Toby said, "I'll drive," and went around to take over.

Lyons tiredly observed, "It went like clockwork. I never saw such a precision damn hit."

"It went great," Bolan agreed.

"Think he'll take the bait?"

"Sooner or later, yeah. One thing's for sure. He has nothing back there to hold him."

Toby had the car in gear and powering toward the junction with the main road, where again they halted. Lyons clapped Bolan's shoulder and got out there. "We'll be watching," he assured the man.

"Let's have a radio check every five minutes," Bolan suggested. "Tell Anders the same."

"Right."

Lyons ran across the road and onto the high ground just beyond.

Bolan and the ladies went on then toward Honolulu.

This was not the end of a mission; it was just the beginning. The Executioner and SOG-3 were gunning for a marked trail to King Fire.

13: Firetrack

The blitz on Chung's stronghold at Kalihi had been designed primarily to roust the guy and get him running—as scared as possible. That strategy had produced an unqualified success in the basic movement. The stronghold was gone, the roust therefore assured. The basic question remaining had to do with how far and how scared the general would run in his reaction to the stunning assault.

The Bolan strategy was an exercise in psychological warfare, built upon three key points:

Hit the enemy with stunning power and devastating results, thus forging the idea of an awesome opponent who could strike at will and with apparent impunity;

Plant the idea in the enemy's tumbling mind that this same opponent was targeted on the family treasures, and that he knew where they were kept;

Keep the enemy under close surveillance and play to his reaction when he sprang to the defense of those treasures.

Bolan had smashed the stronghold and carefully implanted a fear that he might know the secrets of King

Fire—also the hint that he meant to strike there next. He had been careful not to overplay with swaggering threats or overly obvious cues. He had simply dropped the name at a moment of humiliated defeat for a man whose cultural traditions had programmed him for the psychological influences of that curious Asian syndrome called "losing face."

Bolan had dealt with those influences before, in another war with a similar enemy.

He could not, of course, know the depth and width of Chung's probable reaction. He could only wait and watch—perhaps prodding a bit—and hope that point three of the strategy would provide some measure of positive yield—and this is precisely what he was doing.

He had pre-positioned Tommy Anders on high ground overlooking the stronghold for a binocular watch of the immediate post-strike reaction.

Lyons had dropped off to monitor the junction with the main highway which could take the rousted remains of the Chung cadre west toward Honolulu or eastward through the mountains via Wilson Tunnel and on to windward. A vehicle was stashed for Lyons, in case the track led east.

Bolan had dropped off one mile west of the junction, where another vehicle had been planted for his use, and he sent the girls on to Honolulu and another holding point.

First, however, he had assured himself that Smiley Dublin had recovered from her post-blitz attack of nerves and that she was functioning as a member of the team.

"I'm okay," she'd insisted pluckily. "Those tears were purgative." She had smiled, then, and added with a mischievous gleam: "Thanks, I really needed that."

"We need you, too, Smiley," he told her. "Where do you think Chung will go now?"

"You're hoping he will go to the big island, aren't you?"

He nodded affirmatively. "That's the idea. It's where the marbles are."

"If he does, he'll probably send for the helicopter. Flora and Dominick were in for a conference a few hours ago. I believe they're stationed over there. They always come by helicopter. Twice during the past month, the general has been picked up by that same chopper. It's probably company owned. Red with white markings. I never got close enough to see the registry number."

"How big?"

"Oh—five or six passenger, I'd say."

"That could be a help," Toby commented. "We could canvass the suspected area and try to find someone who has seen the thing coming and going. Maybe the FAA could give us a clue. All civil aircraft have to be regularly serviced, certified and all that."

"It's something to keep in mind," Bolan agreed. "But only if all else fails. I don't want to tip our hand. Blundering around with a lot of obvious questions could freeze the whole show."

"I suppose that's true," Toby admitted.

Bolan asked the other girl, "How long was the general gone, on these chopper trips?"

"Overnight, both times," was the reply. "The point is, Mack, if he sends for the helicopter, what good is this track plan of yours?"

"He can't send for it from the stronghold," Bolan explained. "I took out all his communications. That's why I asked: where will he go now?"

Smiley replied, "Remember the man with all the

96

teeth you asked about last night? He has a beach house between Waikiki and Prince Kuhio Beach, over near Diamond Head."

"You've been there?"

"Uh huh. It's where I met Chung for the first few times, before we started playing housey together. I could take you there. But I don't know the address and I wouldn't know how to direct you."

"You're sure you could find it, though?"

"Yes. I'll know the place when I see it."

Bolan pondered that bit of information for a moment before asking the other federal lady, "Is your plane ready to fly, Toby?"

She replied, "Sure. It's always ready."

"Okay, we'll try that if you're both game. Toby, get airborne and maintain position around Diamond Head. Keep your eyes open for that chopper and stay alert on our radio frequency. Follow our play if you can, and stay in touch."

"What about me?" Smiley asked.

"Sure you're ready?"

"Just try it without me," she replied solemnly. "This *is* my case, you know. I opened it. I mean to be here when it's closed."

Bolan grinned at her and said, "Okay. Drop Toby off at the airport, then go straight to Chung's beach house. Have a story ready, in case he shows up there. It should run something like this: I dropped off, out here in the country, and ordered you to keep going. You're scared, confused, didn't know what else to do —so you've come to the beach house hoping to find Chung there. If toothy is there and Chung isn't—when you get there, I mean—play the story on him and sit tight until it becomes obvious that Chung is not going

97

to show. Beat it back to the hotel and sit tight until we contact you."

"I don't like it," Toby protested. "It's back into the fire with Smiley. I thought the idea was to get her *out*."

"It's okay," Smiley said. "I want to do it."

"Toby's right," Bolan said grimly. "I wanted you out. I still do. I believe we can hack it without you, from this point on. But, like you said, it *is* your game. You have a right. And if the track backfires, you're still our best weapon. You could failsafe it for us. Chung likes you. If you do make contact with him and it appears that he is not running to the cues, I believe you could say the right thing to get him running where we want."

She smiled. "I think I could."

Bolan said, "It gets stickier. When the guy heads for the homestand, we need to have you right there beside him."

"Why?" Toby flared. "Why keep her in the middle?"

"Could you manage it?" Bolan asked the girl in the hot seat.

She replied, "In view of—yes, I think so. I believe he'd want to protect me personally, if he thought . . ."

Bolan handed her a cigarette lighter. "Keep this on you, then. It's a miniature radio beacon. It's also a functioning cigarette lighter. If we should lose visual contact, we can maintain the track on audibles."

"How do I activate it?"

"Just light it, the beacon will become operative. You can't shut it down. Has a twelve-hour power life, so don't activate it until you think it's time."

Smiley grimaced and said, "Okay. So I'm wired and ready."

Bolan kissed them both and sent them on their way with the admonition, "Play it tight."

"Listen to Captain Loose," Toby Ranger said, with a wink at the other girl.

And then they were gone.

The thing was in motion.

Anders, from his eagle perch behind the stronghold, reported, "They've given up on the fire. Total loss. Looks like they're getting ready to pull out. They're collecting bodies and weapons, pulling it all together for a clean departure. Hell of a lot of casulties down there."

And, moments later came this report: "Two cars away. Limousines. Six men in the first, looks like a gun crew—some of Topacetti's boys. Chung is in the second car with four other Chinese—driver and three bodyguards, I guess."

Bolan replied, "Okay. Make your scramble and be ready for a track east."

"Roger. Scrambling."

Lyons came in. "Got that. Stand by."

Bolan cautioned him, "Stay clear, Carl. If they're coming my way, give them a thirty-second jump before your start."

"Wilco."

Bolan's vehicle was poised atop a low ridge overlooking the Likelike Highway, a four-lane arterial which traversed the island via the Kalihi Valley. He was playing the odds, gambling on the higher probability that Chung would be heading toward Honolulu rather than to windward. Anders, backdropping on the reverse track, was falling back to play the lower scale of probability. Lyons, with his vehicle at the pivot point, was poised to follow the play either way. Bolan himself had a special role. He was the "kicker"

99

—and his role was to reinforce the psychological overtones of the rout, with a not-so-gentle prod toward paydirt.

Lyon's next communique was, then, a welcome one. "Okay, Kicker, they're all yours," he reported soberly. "Coming at you in close order. Confirming, the general is in the rear vehicle. No other traffic from this direction. It's all yours."

Bolan replied, "Great. Pivot and Backhaul, close on this position—but give it room to develop."

Anders and Lyons both acknowledged the instructions.

The kicker hefted an automatic weapon, made it ready, and walked to the overlook.

It was a perfectly slotted track, embankments to either side. Range, about fifty yards. Visibility, excellent. Situation, beautiful.

Yeah, a perfect shooting gallery.

With just a pinch of luck, the general could get kicked all the way to King Fire.

And they came in right on the numbers, moving sedately at the legal speed limit, running about six carlengths apart—a big crew wagon leading and loaded with glum-faced Mafia torpedoes.

Cheer up, boys—the worst is yet to come.

Bolan stepped to the firing line, in full view of the approaching vehicles, and gave the leading car a long burst from the chattergun, zipping it from bumper to bumper, shattering glass and punching ragged holes from stem to stern along the right side of the big car as it entered the slot.

The heavy vehicle careened and heeled to starboard on collapsing wheels. It went immediately into a sidewise skid, recovered momentarily, then whipped about in its own spilling moisture and slid backwards for

100

several hundred feet before erupting into flames and plummeting off into a deep ravine.

The Chung vehicle had meanwhile quickly reacted to the situation, burning rubber in the emergency slow-down and weaving from lane to lane in an effort to avoid the death plunge of the other car. The driver lost control as his own wheels came into contact with the gas-oil spillage, but the forward motion had slowed sufficiently to preclude a disastrous mishap. They spun off the pavement and came to a gentle halt with the rear of the vehicle wedged against the embankment on the far side of the road. Machine gun fire was spitting at Bolan from a front window, but the angle was bad and the gunner was having trouble bringing an effective track to bear.

Bolan returned the fire but purposefully with little effect. He wanted them running, not burning.

The general was barely visible in the back seat, huddled behind two other men.

The vehicle roared out of its stalled position and fishtailed across in front of Bolan, machine gun still chattering and chopping at the rocks above his head.

Bolan had abandoned his own chattergun in preference of the precision targeting capability of the awesome AutoMag—the piece which Bolan called "Big Thunder."

The big silver gun was extended and tracking in a two-hand hold as the swinging vehicle found its purchase in a squealing acceleration. Bolan coolly squeezed off two rounds and watched the general's human shield dissolve as the heavy .44s blasted into the car and sent shock waves reverberating along the slot. He got a flash view of a frightened face in the background of that exploding flesh—and there were also, Bolan hoped, shock waves streaking through a

101

Chinese general's soul as he huddled there in the gore of his bodyguards.

The vehicle was clear now, off and running again, reaching the point where the first car had plunged off the road just as the latter's final demise was announced by a thunderous explosion and a whoofing fireball.

Bolan sent a couple more rounds from his own Thunder punching through the rear window of the fleeing car, just for punctuation. Then he thumbed on his transmitter and reported to his companions along the backtrack. "Okay, he's kicked. Activate the track plan and we'll see how far."

Lyons' vehicle was already in sight. "Roger, and on track," he replied.

"Just past the junction and closing," reported Anders.

Yeah. The track was on. All the way to hell, maybe.

14: With Sad Regrets

Harold Brognola had been a minor official in the U.S. Justice Department's organized crime division when Mack Bolan began his blitzing warfare against the American underworld. He had been on the scene in Los Angeles when Bolan smashed the California crime family of Julian DiGeorge, and a sort of tense cooperative effort had been quietly forged between the two gangbusters during that early campaign.

The illicit relationship between the two had escalated in direct proportion to Bolan's war effort. Brognola's official status in the department had soared to a rather impressive level of command, also as an indirect result of the relationship. Ironically enough, Brognola himself had been given prime responsibility for bringing Mack Bolan to "justice." Big deal. In Brognola's mind, the only true justice for the guy would be a hero's welcome in the national capital.

Brognola had once quietly campaigned for official sanction of Bolan's war. He had even succeeded in pulling a package together which included total amnesty and a secret Presidential mandate to continue the war—a license, in other words. All the guy had to do was to agree to accept governmental direction, with its necessary checks and balances—and the damned, doomed, proud bastard had turned it down flat.

"Thanks," he'd told Brognola in Miami, "but I'll do it my way."

That decision had been the one to seal his doom. For awhile there, the heat from the federal government had been somewhat diminished, thanks to Brognola's quiet intercessions. But then the war drums had begun to roll atop Capitol Hill and the pressures to apprehend Mack Bolan became intense. Naturally and understandably, many of the nation's lawmakers saw the Bolan thing as an affront and a direct menace to the American system of justice.

Brognola saw it differently. He had been fighting the frustrating and hamstrung battle against the creeping menace of organized crime for many years. A guy like Bolan was a godsend. He was powerful, incorruptible, totally dedicated to the war and absolutely committed to a system of ethics which provided its own checks and balances.

Yet, Brognola himself had succumbed to those pressures, very briefly, and he'd personally gone gunning for the Executioner in Las Vegas—albeit with sad regret. Luckily he had failed, and Brognola had vowed at the time that it would not, dammit, happen again. He had an oath of office to think about, sure, but there was also a strong sense of rightness that dictated Hal Brognola's official conscience. He would discharge the duties of his office, sure, but with all other values firmly intact—and he would give Mack Bolan as much operating room as possible. Hal Brognola was no damn computer punch-card. Neither was Mack Bolan.

But the poor guy was doomed, and Brognola knew that for sure. The federal government was not ruled by any one man. The government was a machine, and that machine would sooner or later ingest Mack Bolan and his valiant war. If the feds didn't stop him, then some local police department would—if his natural enemies did not get to him first.

Bolan himself must know that, Brognola was thinking as he stepped out of the official vehicle with Lieutenant Patterson of HPD. They had come directly from the airport to the scene of the latest suspected Bolan strike.

"This is it," Patterson announced, with a gesture toward the smoking ruin of what had obviously once been a splendid country estate. "We found it just this way. Apparently they loaded up their dead and wounded and beat it. Wasn't just a fire. The place was definitely *hit*. Bullets and shrapnel are imbedded everywhere. And look at that wall. Bomb squads say the gutted car at the gate there was carrying some heavy explosive inside the grill. Probably impact-triggered. He simply rolled the car down the hill and jumped out before the impact."

Brognola grunted and stepped through the hole in the wall.

God, what a hit!

"You're right," he said quietly.

"Eh?"

"Bolan's been here. What you see here is practically a signature."

"Well, he'd scrawled his name on a few more places on this island before he got here."

"What'd you say this place is?" Brognola absently inquired.

"Cultural exchange mission or some such. Obviously a front."

"Obvious before the fact?"

"Frankly, I'd never heard of the place," the lieutenant admitted. "But I can't speak for the entire department."

"I suggest that you start," Brognola said quietly.

"Look—it's only been—what?—eight or ten hours since the guy started this rampage. My tac force has reps from the entire department, but—"

"Eight or ten hours is sometimes the entire span of a Bolan operation. If you mean to stop this guy, it has to be an all-hands effort. The guy *hits* and *gits*. He could already be gone."

They were stepping carefully through the mess in the west garden, pausing here and there to scrutinize some particularly interesting piece of evidence as the conversation continued. A horde of cops and firemen were on the scene, patiently sifting the ruins.

Patterson said, "He's still on the island, I'm confident of that. We have it sealed. And we do have an all-hands effort going. I mean, life does go on, you know—wc still have a whole island to police just as though this guy had never blown in on us—but I can tell you that not a cop in this county is lying on his butt right now. We even have the reserves called up."

Brognola had halted to kneel beside a strange apparatus which was partially buried beneath a crumbled wall of the house. "Statewide alert?" he inquired.

"As wide as it can get," Patterson replied. "We have a unique police situation in Hawaii. There is no state police, you know—nothing that even corresponds to it. Honolulu County covers the entire island of Oahu. We got it all, and it's a big area—six hundred square miles and about eighty percent of the total state population. Hawaii County, that's the big island, has the only other strong police department in the state, but they get most of the land area with less than ten percent of the population. Maui and Kauai do what they can with what they have, but I'm afraid that's not

106

much. There is a good spirit of cooperation between the islands but—what's that you've got there?"

"I'm not sure," Brognola mused. He was tugging a metallic framework from beneath the pile of rubble. "Looks like a uh . . ."

"Of course our prime effort," Patterson resumed, "is aimed at containing the guy on Oahu. Sooner or later we're going to close the net on the guy. It's just a matter of time." He dropped to one knee and ran an exploratory finger along Brognola's find. "I've seen some big kites," he commented. "The Chinese here really make some fancy ones. But I've never seen—"

Brognola grunted, "Here we go," as he pulled a scorched scrap of nylon from the framework. "It's no kite. Look at this bar that runs along here—shit!—know what that was? A damn glider, one of those one-man deals that . . ."

The fed stood up suddenly and cast a thoughtful gaze toward the wrecked wall.

Patterson fidgeted and said, "What, uh . . . ?"

"Hell, I don't know," Brognola replied thoughtfully. He stepped off toward the pond, then halted and craned his neck in an inspection of the surrounding terrain.

"What is it?" Patterson called over.

"This is no place for sport soaring. But *he* might. The damn guy just might!"

"Might what?"

"Don't ask yet, I'm trying to set this in my head. How much do you know about gliders and soaring?"

"Not a damn thing," the lieutenant admitted, walking out to join the other man. "But if you're thinking— I showed you, he blasted in through the gate."

"Blasted, right," Brognola agreed. "That doesn't necessarily mean that he blasted *in*. Something you

107

have to understand, Greg. This guy Bolan has a military mind. He's a tactical genius. If this place was as well defended as I'm thinking it was—look, the guy's no superman. I mean, he bleeds when he's hit, just like anyone. He doesn't simply storm in and depend on luck to see him through. He's got a mind like . . ."

"Then he had to have accomplices," Patterson decided.

"Maybe. Maybe not."

"Put it together," Patterson argued. "Without an accomplice, there's no way. You're thinking a diversion at the entrance, a sneak attack over the rear from the air. That spells out to more than a one-man attack."

Brognola suddenly threw his hands into the air and said, "You're right. It was a dumb thought to start with. He blasted in."

The lieutenant was giving the fed an odd look. "Well, wait," he said slowly. "Let's think about it. If he has accomplices, we should—"

"Naw, naw," the fed interrupted. "It was just a wild hunch, a shiver thought. Bolan works alone, period. The glider is a coincidence. No saying how long it's been here. Probably belonged to whoever lived here—a soaring enthusiast, probably. Let's take another look at that wall."

The HPD man was still giving Brognola the fish-eye gaze, but he went on to the wall without pursuing the subject further. The guy was plenty sharp, though—that much was obvious. And he knew that Hal Brognola was lying through his federal teeth. Mack Bolan, in all probability, had *not* been alone on this hit.

And the very possible identity of those accomplices

108

immediately presented to the federal mind had set the hairs twanging in Brognola's nose.

This one was going to be a son of a bitch, for sure.

A moment later he suggested to the cop from HPD: "We'd better get back to town and set the defense. I'll want to activate some military units, too. I can do that. Bolan is still army property and he's classified as a deserter."

"I'd rather not get into that," Patterson protested.

"You're into it already. The guy is gunning for a foreign national, and a damned sensitive one, at that. I brought orders straight from the White House. Believe it, Greg, you're into it already."

And so, albeit with sad regret, was Hal Brognola.

Yeah. The poor, proud bastard was doomed. Brognola had his orders, from the highest. The Executioner was to die in Hawaii.

15: Running Hot

The three chase cars had alternated the close track on the Chung vehicle, with first one and then the other surging forward to maintain visual contact until the target car entered the interchange with H1, the interstate route through Honolulu, also known as Lunalilo Freeway. Bolan was riding point at that juncture, and he quickly signaled the others to close immediately.

"It's a bumper banger here on Lunalilo," he reported. "We're through the interchange and running south in heavy traffic. Better close it in and maintain hot visual."

Lyons and Anders acknowledged the instructions and both were jockeying about in Bolan's wake by the time he reached the even denser traffic at the Pali Highway junction.

Lyons suggested, "If he's headed for Prince Kuhio Beach, he'll probably run the Lunalilo to somewhere down around the Waialae or Kapiolani exits. Maybe I should go on around and let him overtake me just north of Waialae."

Bolan replied, "Okay, go—no, hold it!"

The car ahead with the shattered rear window was creeping far right and signaling an exit at the Ward Avenue offramp.

Lyons commented, "So he's playing it cute."

"That's taking it the hard way," Anders chimed in. "He's probably angling toward Kalakaua and a drag along Waikiki. I sure wouldn't try that in a bullet-ridden car."

"We're running it too hot," Bolan decided. "Carl—take him from here. I'll go on to the next exit and circle back. Tom—keep Carl in sight."

Lyons and Anders edged into the exit and Bolan shot on past in the through lane, then immediately started his blinker and made preparations for exiting at the next opportunity.

A moment later, Lyons reported, "Running south on Beretania."

Bolan replied, "Good. I'll be coming down on the auditorium exit. Keep me cued."

"Right. Academy of Arts coming up." Then: "Turning west on Pensacola."

Anders suggested, "Try for a pickup at Kalakaua and Kapiolani, Mack. I'm still betting on a Waikiki drag."

"I don't like it," Bolan groused. "Beretania to Kalakaua would've been the best shot at the beach. You guys double-team it and ride him hot."

Lyons said, "Turning onto Kapiolani now. I just got a shiver that says Ala Moana." A moment later: "Yep, yep. That's where we're headed. We're on Piikoi, running toward the park."

"Yacht harbor!" Bolan shot back.

"Could be. What do you say, Tommy?"

"We could still end up on Kalakaua," the comic replied. "But, yeah, I'd have to vote for the boats. Looks like Kuhio Beach is a strike-out."

"Okay," Bolan told them, "I'm closing along Atkinson Drive. Give me your mark as you pass that point."

111

"We're on Ala Moana," Lyons reported a moment later. "Running south."

"Roger."

"Atkinson coming up. Stand by. *Mark*—still running south. Ala Wai dead ahead."

Bolan replied, "Okay, I caught your passage. I'm about ten seconds off your tail. Fall back and give Tom the heat."

"Moving up," Anders immediately reported.

From Lyons: "Have him in sight?"

"Got him. Drop off."

Bolan said, "Play him close, Tom. I'm coming around now. Okay, Ala Moana. What's your position, Carl?"

"Approaching the inlet bridge."

"Roger. Tom?"

"Kaiser Hospital and here we go. It's the yachts, all right."

"Lay back but keep them in sight."

"Roger."

"Close it up, Carl."

"Right, closing."

From Anders: "They're going straight in. It's a score. Target is now in the parking area. I'm hauling up."

"Carl, follow them in!"

"End of track, Mack. Where do we go from here? Or have you started walking on water, also?"

"Just keep them in sight, dammit, and get a good eyeball on their boat."

"I have them in sight," Lyons reported with a sigh.

A female voice cut into the three-way radio conversation with a bright comment: "What's all the panic down there?"

Bolan pulled his vehicle into the slot beside Anders,

112

stepped out with a tired grin, and thumbed on his transmitter. "What's your position, Toby?"

"Look up. Straight up. See the pretty silver wings?"

Bolan chuckled. "Yep, and they're a sight for heavy eyes, m'lady. Welcome to the chase."

"Some chase," she replied. "New subject. Something funny may be happening with Smiley. Her beacon is beeping. Isn't it a bit soon for that?"

Bolan quickly reached into the vehicle for his monitor and turned it on. He was receiving a strong pulse. "It is," he told the lady upstairs. "Can you track a boat from up there?"

"I can track a peanut shell if you boys will just point it out as it leaves the harbor. What about Smiley?"

"You're right, it's too soon. I'll check it out. Toby, it will be a few minutes before these people can get underway. Take a quick run right now, straight out to sea, and give me a leg fix on that beacon."

"On my way," she reported, as the little single-engine plane banked off seaward.

Anders, standing beside Bolan, asked, "What's wrong with Smiley?"

"Maybe nothing," Bolan told him. "All I need is a quick fix to verify the course to her beacon. Then I can drive right to it, on my monitor alone. I'll be leaving Chung to you guys for now. Let Carl watch him onto the boat. Meanwhile, you beat it up to the office and get one for yourselves."

"Hell, these are all privately owned boats, I think," Anders said. "I mean, I don't know if you can *rent* one."

"Rent, borrow, or commandeer—get one," Bolan replied. "A fast one, with inter-island capability."

"What about you? How will you . . . ?"

"I'll have to work it by ear. If we lose contact, check back with your hotel every hour until we contact. Don't close on Chung. Give him rope and let him go where he will. Just make damn sure you know where that is."

"Sure," Anders said. "Hey. Be careful."

"You too," Bolan replied.

The voice of Carl Lyons came through the radio. "Okay, he's boarding. Chung only. Something odd here. A man is missing."

"I don't read that," Bolan said.

"Me either. There was a guy in front with the driver. He got out somewhere before here."

Bolan said, "Dammit!" to Anders. To Lyons, via the radio, he asked, "You're sure that's Chung you're looking at?"

"It's him," came the positive reply. "Stepping aboard the *Pele Phoenix,* right now. It's a big one."

Bolan replied, "Stay right there. Tom's getting a boat. Did you hear the gig with Toby?"

"I heard. Good luck."

"Right, and back at you. Watch it."

Anders mused, "The *Pele Phoenix,* eh? There's a fire goddess for you—with wings, yet, rising from ashes. How symbolic can you get?"

Toby Ranger cut off Bolan's response to that. She reported, "Mack, this range should be okay for tri-angulation. I'm getting a compass line that cuts the island just north of Diamond Head."

Bolan was consulting his own monitor as she spoke. He told her, "Okay, I got it. Looks like Kuhio, all right. I'm moving out. Maintain the track with Tom and Carl."

"Right. Be careful."

114

Mack Bolan was always careful, especially when a precious life might be hanging in the balance.

And already he was on the move again, running hot along an electronic track—for life, this time, for a precious life.

Yes, for damn sure.

The *Pele Phoenix,* eh?

Bolan's soul groaned. He should not have sent that girl back into the fires. But he had. And now the hell-grounds were yawning wide.

16: Kill Order

Brognola and Patterson returned to Honolulu via police helicopter, arriving at the tactical operations center just in time to hear the report from a surveillance unit at Ala Wai Harbor.

"A man with federal credentials just commandeered a cruiser from the harbormaster here. Doesn't fit our subject's description, but the orders are to report any unusual movement. I call this unusual."

Patterson yelled from the doorway, "Tell 'im to stop that guy!"

"Reconsider that, Greg!" Brognola snapped. "That could be one of my people!"

The lieutenant turned a see-all, saying-nothing gaze upon the fed as he countermanded the order. "Belay it," he instructed the tac dispatcher. "Get a chopper over there. I want full details, and I want air surveillance on that cruiser!"

To Brognola he growled, "You and I better get some cards on the table, mister," then he spun away into the glass-enclosed cubicle which served as his office.

Brognola came in with a somewhat chastened face, lighting a cigar and dropping into a chair with a weary grunt.

Patterson reminded his VIP visitor, "You didn't tell me you had operators here."

116

"You didn't ask," Brognola lamely explained.

"Cooperation works both ways. I give you an open book. You give me a wink and a giggle. That's not going to work."

"I told you, Greg," the fed quietly replied, "that the White House is directly interested in this problem. Of course I have operatives in the field. But it's only indirectly related to the Bolan hunt. It's, uh, very sensitive."

"Don't pull that national security bull on me, bub," Patterson said huffily. "And don't try to pull rank on me, either. My salary is paid by the city and county of Honolulu. I'm not here to defend the country but to uphold the law in this political subdivision. You come clean with me or get your ass out of here."

"You're a tough bastard," Brognola commented, grinning.

"You don't make it in this department any other way," the lieutenant retorted. "I tried it the other way with you, mister."

"I *could* pull rank, you know," the fed quietly pointed out. "One phone call would put your ass on the sidewalk looking in and wondering what happened. But I don't operate that way."

"How *do* you operate?" Patterson asked, glowering at his visitor.

"To the fullest extent possible toward noninterference. To the maximum extent allowable toward complete confidence and cooperation. But don't get tough with me, Greg. I'll tell you what I can. You carry on with that, or I'll get someone in here who will."

"So maybe I'm a paper tiger," the lieutenant said with a grimace. "What can you tell me?"

A uniformed cop interrupted the set-to with a type-

117

written report which he placed in Patterson's hands. "Came in a minute ago," he said, giving Brognola a sidewise glance as he went out.

"What is it?" Brognola inquired, interested.

"Another page in the open book," Patterson replied. "Patrol unit just found a bullet-riddled Cadillac in a ravine just off Likelike Highway. Two miles west of you-know-where." He passed the report to the fed, adding, "Plus six cremated bodies. This boy of yours plays mighty rough games . . . or somebody does."

"Chase car, maybe?" Brognola commented, reading the report and probing Patterson's reading at the same time.

"Sounds that way, doesn't it?"

"Set it up for me," Brognola requested.

"Okay. The guy hits the joint in the valley—with or without accomplices. There's a—"

"Let's say without."

"Okay, the guy hits. There's a hot pursuit. The guy sees this. He comes onto a blind curve with a good lead, quickly pulls over, leaves the car and runs up a ridge, meets the pursuit at the curve with a blazing machine gun. End of chase."

"That's my read," the fed said. "No identification of the victims, though. We're assuming a lot, maybe. Could just as easy be the other way. A chase, catch, chastisement. End of the guy plus accomplices."

"You don't really believe it, though," Patterson said.

"No. Just trying sizes."

"But you are worried just a little," the lieutenant said, doing some reading of his own.

"Maybe," Brognola admitted. "Just a little."

Patterson depressed an intercom button to growl, "I want the registry make on the Likelike Cadillac as

118

soon as you have it." Then he reminded Brognola, "You were about to tell me something—the earlier discussion."

"Not much, I'm afraid," the fed replied, his eyes still exploring the police report. "You're going to have to take a lot on faith. I've told you all I can with regard to General Loon. And now you know that I have people working the problem. The curtain falls right there. It's a mere coincidence that Bolan has blitzed into the picture. My superiors want Bolan as bad as you do. But we cannot allow the Bolan hunt to interfere with our Loon problem."

"Loon, spoon—I don't give a shit," Patterson growled unhappily. "We've got a police problem on this island. If I find out that your people are aiding and abetting a fugitive who is already a mass murderer in this jurisdiction, then I'm going to come down hard on them."

"Why would you think such a thing?" Brognola asked mildly.

"Look, Hal, dammit—Honolulu is not exactly Timbuctu. We're a part of the Fifty, remember. We get the usual magazines and syndicated columns. The whole damn country is wondering if Mack Bolan isn't operating under some secret government sponsorship. Your credibility is a matter of public discussion, Mr. Brognola. If you *are* backing this guy, and you *do* have operators on the island—and it appears that the Kalihi Valley hit was more than a one-man operation—now tell me, *federale*, why would I think such a thing?"

"You're a tactless shit, aren't you," the fed said glumly.

"I try very hard to be."

Brognola sighed and said, "Push that telephone over here." He produced a card from his wallet and placed

119

a call. Then, his eyes steadily on the HPD lieutenant throughout the exchange, he announced, "This is Justice Two. Connect me with the duty officer, NSC Urgent."

Patterson nervously lit a cigarette while Brognola awaited the connection.

"Duty officer? Give me your identity number, please."

The fed jotted a number on a pad, eyes still fixed on Patterson.

"Thank you. This is Justice Two. Please record this NSC authority number: one geneva six delta alpha three. This is an activate order, file Justice thirteen four twenty-one, authentication zebra zebra seven zero. Will you check that, please."

Brognola continued to gaze at the Honolulu cop while awaiting some response from the other end of the phone connection. Patterson puffed on his cigarette and stared right back. "So I'm impressed," he growled.

Brognola winked solemnly and immediately resumed the telephone conversation. "Very good. This is an Activate. Line One. Ten CID, five-zero Military Police, two helicopter units on ten-minute alert. More to follow. Stand by."

He covered the transmitter with a hand to ask Patterson, "Anything you want?"

The cop sneered and dropped his gaze.

Brognola chuckled. "Captain? Yes. Line Two. Stand by Alert. One Air Tactical squadron, one naval amphibious support unit, one company airborne infantry. Line Three. Immediate and continuous electronic search, all nonmilitary radio channels, intercept and monitor per File Justice thirteen four twenty-one for intelligence evaluation, immediate report all positive results. Line Four negative, Line Five negative. That is all. Please repeat."

Brognola listened attentively to the verification readback, then he gave the number of the phone from which he was calling and added, "If I am not here, contact me via Lieutenant Greg Patterson, Honolulu Police Tactical Force. Right. Thank you, Captain."

He hung up, again caught Patterson's eye, and said, "Credibility gap, eh. Get screwed, Lieutenant. That was a Kill Order. And the name at the top of that file is Bolan, Mack Samuel, Master Sergeant, USA. And the best damned man I've ever known."

"Sorry," Patterson murmured. "Whoever said police work was for tea drinkers."

"Nobody I've ever heard," Brognola agreed.

"NSC," the cop mused. "National Security Council, right?"

"Right."

"Is it on the level?"

"Do you have an undercover general from Peking in your town?"

Patterson sighed. "So I've gotten used to wearing iron pants. I apologize. But . . . how come *you?* Why not the FBI or the CIA or some other roseblush outfit?"

"It's a long and sordid story," Brognola said. "Remind me to tell you some time—say, in about the year nineteen-ninety."

"Things are getting sticky in Washington, aren't they?"

"Sticky you never dreamed of," the fed replied. "Speaking of tea drinkers . . . You wouldn't have any stashed about, would you?"

Patterson chuckled, opened a drawer, and replied, "The best PanAm has to offer. Name your poison."

"Plain rotgut would do."

The lieutenant slid over a single-service bottle of bourbon, then selected a vodka for himself. "I guess this makes us drinking buddies," he said, then tossed it down raw. Without so much as a recovery breath, he asked, "When do you loose the dogs on Bolan?"

"Soon as you give me a relative fix on him," the fed replied. He belted the bourbon, made a face, and commented, "Maybe tea would be better, at that," then soberly added: "When you drink a man down, though, it doesn't seem fitting any other way."

"You really like the guy, don't you?" Patterson commented quietly.

"Yeah."

"I could see it. Out in Kalihi a while ago. It shows."

"How'd it look a couple minutes ago?"

"Oh, official. Brutally official."

"I was bleeding inside," the fed admitted. "Still am. Yeah. I like the guy. Very much."

The uniformed cop reentered with another formal report and handed it over to Patterson.

"Maybe I do, too," the lieutenant said, folding the paper and dropping it to the desk. "The Cadillac is registered to Lou Topacetti."

Brognola grunted, "As mean a hood as ever left the Windy City."

"Right. So that was a gun crew, all other bets off. Bolan whacked them. I don't get it, Hal. This angle on General Loon, I mean—Chung. What are these guys trying to pull here?"

"God, I don't know, I really don't," Brognola replied wearily. "I betcha I know a guy who does know, though. And here we are, you and me, plotting to whack him back."

"You want to talk to Oliveras?"

"Not even through your mouth, no. Fuck that guy. Why didn't Bolan finish him, huh? One will get you ten that he never spends a whole day in jail. Why didn't Bolan take him clean?"

"Said he was saving him. Even tipped me about one of our own cops, who Bolan says has a contract from Chung to finish the job."

"Maybe that's the guy we should be talking to."

"Don't think I wouldn't like to. He's blown off somewhere. I have a detail looking for him. You're such an expert on Mack Bolan. Why would he be saving a misery merchant like Fatty Oliveras?"

"I couldn't say," the fed replied. "Unless he figures the guy to know something important."

"Which means," Patterson deduced, "that Bolan could be figuring to hit his pigeon again."

"Could be," Brognola agreed. "I'm sure you're covering that possibility."

"I am."

"Still priming the pump, aren't you," Brognola said, smiling. "You think I'm holding out on you?"

"Sure you are."

The fed laughed. The cop laughed.

Only because it beat the hell out of crying.

Brognola said, "I am bone weary."

"Tie it up," the cop suggested. "Have a hotel?"

"No. Don't want one. Couldn't sleep, anyway. All the little phantoms come out and begin their dance soon as I close my eyes. Haven't slept well for a long time, Greg."

"Like I said," Patterson commented, sighing, "it's no business for tea drinkers." He opened the drawer and slid another bourbon to the man from Washington. "Put the phantoms to sleep," he suggested. "Works for me every time."

123

"Won't work on Bolan," Brognola said. "Nothing works on that guy. He's out there, right now—somewhere—drinking blood by the buckets. And it's that blood, friend cop, that you and I should be drinking instead of this rotgut."

"Knock it off," Patterson growled. "You'll have me doubting my own deepest convictions. Mack Bolan may be a great guy in your book—but he's wrong. You know that. He's wrong. That's not the way to go."

"Never said it was," Brognola muttered. "But it's *his* way. And it's a lot more effective, friend cop, than yours and mine."

"Bull."

"He's never shot a cop. Never hurt an innocent party. Never asked for a damn thing from the likes of you and me—and doesn't expect anything. Turned down a license, even."

"That's true, then."

"Oh, yeah. Most of what you hear is true. The proud shit! Lives in perpetual hell. Can't let down for a second, no rest—I don't know how the hell he does it. You have any idea what it must *take* just to keep putting one foot after the other that way—day after day, week after week, on and on and on? Who can he trust? Who can he depend on? What's the guy got? Can you tell me that? What the hell has he *got?*"

The lieutenant was silent for a moment before gruffly commenting, "He called it, man. He can call it off, just as easy."

"On-and-off switch, eh?" Brognola said. "Sure, it sounds easy. When's the last time you turned your switch off, cop?"

"Bull."

"Sure. Bull. No switches, right? We're going to get that guy, Greg. You or me, or both together. We're going to whack the one guy who has the handle on the mob situation in this country. Makes a lot of sense, doesn't it."

The lieutenant heaved to his feet and went to the window.

Brognola smoked silently for a minute, then picked up a clipboard of tac bulletins and began going through them.

The hands of the big clock on the wall moved slowly but relentlessly toward the countdown on the life of Mack Bolan.

Reports continued to arrive. Brognola read them aloud and added them to the accumulation on the clipboard. Patterson remained at the window, silent, hands shoved deeply into pants pockets.

Then the big one came. Brognola read it in a flat voice: "Sustained gunfire reports, vicinity Kuhio Beach. Patrol units responding. Tac Force alerted, all units in Sector Four proceeding under extreme caution."

Patterson wheeled away from the window. "That could be it," he growled. "Coming?"

"Not in person," Brognola replied in a saddened voice.

He had the telephone to his ear—had evidently been placing the call during the reading of the report.

"This is Justice Two. Connect me with the duty officer, NSC Immediate."

Patterson ran out.

To hell with the phantoms.

The big cop from HPD had a Kill Order of his own to fill.

17: Beach Party

In generalizing the location of Chung's beach home away from home, Smiley had said "between Waikiki and Prince Kuhio Beach, over near Diamond Head."

It was quite a generalization. Actually, the entire shoreline from Ala Wai to Diamond Head presents an unbroken, graceful crescent of beautiful beach, and the entire stretch is usually referred to as Waikiki Beach. Down beyond the sprawl of luxury hotels, restaurants, bars, and other trappings of the tourist trade, though, lies that section of Waikiki which has been preserved, more or less, for those who make their homes on the island. Kuhio Beach Park and Kapiolani Park are there with their lovely groves, zoo, aquarium, natatorium, bandshell, public baths, and other facilities for the general public. Inland from Kuhio, across Kalakaua Avenue, are residential streets with exotic names such as Kealohilani, Lilioukalani, and Paoakalani, intertwining with such down-to-earth streets as Cleghorn, Cartwright, and Mountainview.

There are no beach houses per se in this area. The entire stretch of beach is publicly owned and protected from private exploitation or lockouts. Smiley evidently had in mind one of the homes which line the inland streets, and which conceivably could be regarded as beach houses since they do border and are within shouting distance of the public beaches.

In such a jumble, it would have been unlikely that Bolan's electronic box could have led him to the exact house in which he was hoping to find Smiley Dublin alive and well. As it turned out, such precision was not necessary because the radio course led not to the back streets but to the public beach itself—and Bolan found Smiley Dublin, alive and apparently well, strolling the water's edge near a palm grove and abundantly filling the tiniest bikini it had been his pleasure to see in quite a while.

She was not alone, however.

Something that was probably meant to pass as a congenial beach party was in progress there.

A couple of grass-skirted beauties were shaking the hay nearby for the benefit of a cluster of hard-eyed torpedoes who were laboring unsuccessfully to look like innocent tourists having a carefree time.

Back off the water's edge, twenty feet or so into the grove, a roasting pig was turning slowly on a spit above glowing coals, tended by a small group of Oriental gentlemen in gaily-colored shirtsleeves.

A pair of huge outrigger canoes were pulled partially onto the sand, their prows afloat in the surf and moving gently in response to the constant ebb and flow of the Pacific. A Chinese guy wearing a faded Hawaiian loincloth, trying and failing to look like a beach boy, stood guard over the outriggers and a rack of bone-dry surfboards.

At most any other time, the scene would have been set rather well. But not at this time of the morning— not even for the most disorganized of tour guides. It was too late for the solemn assembly to pass as the lingerings of an all-night party and much too early to qualify for the luncheon special.

The park seemed otherwise deserted.

Farther north, toward Waikiki Beach Center, a few surfers were taking a go at the early-morning action while here and there could be seen an occasional stroller.

Bolan had armed himself for heavy combat and left his vehicle far to the rear, making his approach through the groves. At the moment, he was crouched in the foliage not twenty yards from where Smiley played idly with foot impressions in the wet sand at the surf line, studiously willing the girl to look his way.

Giving up on this unproductive line of contact, he waited until the grass-skirted gyrations of the dancing girls shifted gears into muscular destruct, thereby assuring the undivided attention of the would-be tourists, then he tossed a bull's-eye cross on a dead-drop course for the girl in the bikini.

It struck her on the thigh and fell to the sand beside her. She gave no outward reaction whatever, except to step on the medal and press it into the wet sand. A moment later, though, she began moving slowly toward him, keeping to the surf line, continuing to dig playfully at the sand with her toes.

Smiley reached a position directly opposite Bolan's and dropped to one knee, her back to the "party," to make designs in the sand with a finger. "Wow," she declared quietly. "Am I glad to see you."

"What's the gig, Smiley?"

"A small deviation. The general is not coming. We're going to him."

"I'd gathered that much."

"Apparently this has been planned since last night, since just after your first little blast at the general.

Your dawn strike advanced the timetable a bit, that's all. It did cause quite a stir here."

"How'd they get the word?"

"I brought it. Then, a few minutes later, one of Chung's men called from someplace in town. We're to rendezvous at sea."

"Who is *we?*"

"Wang Ho, his staff, and me. Wang's the one with the teeth. I believe he's a rat. I do know he's not planning on taking me all the way."

"How do you know that?"

"I understand the language and I overheard the instructions. I'm to be given the opportunity to swim the Kaiwi Channel, I take it. Swim or sink, you know, with the emphasis on sink."

She was a hell of a gal. Calm, cool, pro all the way.

Bolan said, "Okay, keep moving. Start running at the next grove north. My vehicle is parked just off Ohua street. I'll cover the withdrawal and meet you here."

"Huh-uh. We don't get off that easy."

One of the torpedoes with the hula girls had swung away from the rest of the group to gaze at Smiley, hands on his hips, watching her with a contemplative smile. Bolan warned her, "You're being watched. Spill it quick and careful."

"They've decided that your overt attentions at Kalihi could be the crack in their dam and they're worried now about the exposure. So they're cutting losses and moving the headquarters. Wang is top dog. He transferred a portfolio of sealed documents from a safe in his house, has them now chained to his wrist in an attache case. I caught a remark he made to his chief of staff. It translates to, 'This is where the body is buried'—but he was speaking figuratively. I believe

129

there's political dynamite in those documents. We need them, in case this thing blows into an international confrontation."

Bolan said, "Okay, beat it. I'll get the damn documents."

"You can't do it alone!" she hissed. "I'm here. Use me, dammit."

"How much time do we have?"

"Not much. We're supposed to push off in the outriggers. Rendezvous with a yacht somewhere out beyond the coral reef."

"So what are they waiting for?"

"The yacht, I guess. They're watching for it."

Bolan pondered the situation for a moment as he studied the torpedo who was watching Smiley. The guy seemed about ready to amble over.

"Go wiggle your butt at that gorilla," Bolan decided. "Get a scene going, anything with lots of excitement. Get those people off the beach. And stay the hell away from those canoes."

"What's the move, after that?"

"Just play it to my cues. Go on. The guy's moving this way."

Smiley got to her feet, turned languidly toward the approaching bruiser, and said to him, "What a drag. Aren't you just bored to death?"

"I *was*," the guy replied, grinning.

Smiley laughed and tossed her hips. "Who needs a grass skirt?" she cried, and threw herself into the routine that had stopped shows from San Juan to Las Vegas.

And, yeah, she was something else—something very special. Bolan was reminded again of what that girl had sacrificed to this grim game of cops and robbers. It was a talent which did not appear spontaneously upon every stage in the land—and she very quickly had that entire assemblage of hoods thoroughly captivated by the sensual grace of her dance. The movements carried her off the beach and into the grove with the roasting pig. The show of the hula girls had come to a confused halt as their audience flowed into the grove behind the insinuating motions of their competitor. There was no one to watch them now but the guy in the faded loincloth, and even he was edging closer for a view into the picnic grove.

Bolan had removed his hardware and cached it when he heard Smiley call out, "Give me a beat, come on, with the hand, like this."

The guys were clapping their hands in time and whooping it up when Bolan slipped unnoticed into the water, a small plastic bag gripped in his teeth. He went straight out for depth and circled back, body surfing and allowing the natural motion of the rollers to work him over toward the beach party.

Fifteen seconds at the prows of those canoes was all he wanted—and he got it.

Twenty seconds later he was returning quietly into the concealing foliage at his point of departure and whispering a thanks to his brother, the Pacific.

Those war canoes were now gooped for doomsday, ready to blow upon command from a tiny electronic detonator which rode his ready belt. Small charges, sure, but enough to rip off a couple of bows.

And not a moment too soon.

A large boat with a deep-water hull and pennants flapping from the flying bridge was moving along the coast from the direction of Ala Wai, still a good distance north but within clear sight from Kuhio.

Another one, smaller, sleeker, was moving several

points astern and a quarter-mile or so farther out; the SOG boat, was Bolan's hopeful reading.

Someone at the party had noticed the event, also. A sharp command rang out and the revelry came to an abrupt halt.

Bolan had a glimpse of Smiley Dublin, struggling to get a bikini top adjusted and hovering at the side of a tall Oriental in a flowered Hawaiian shirt. They were moving toward the beach. Another glimpse between the trees provided the identification: it was the toothy one, also wearing a wrist chain attached to a thin briefcase.

Bolan circled to their rear and came in through the trees, a machine-pistol assembled and ready. The Detroit hood, Pete Rodani, was leading a group to one of the outriggers; Martin Pensa, the Cleveland rep, was urging another group toward the other canoe.

Wang Ho and three other Chinese were paused stiffly at the edge of the grove, Smiley in their midst.

It was going to be a hair-splitter, for damn sure.

Bolan stepped into the open and cut sand at their feet with a burst from the chattergun.

The girl took a dive to the side, yelling something at the hula girls as she did so. The Chinese whirled into the confrontation, the realization of doom pulling at those not-so-inscrutable features. A bawling and milling erupted from the water's edge, with a brandishing of arms and a confusion of alarmed commands.

In that split-second of realization, though, hovered the certain knowledge of a stand-off situation. The Chinese were framed directly on the high ground between Bolan and the others.

"Nobody moves!" Bolan yelled, adding emphasis to that situation.

132

Rodani yelled from the boats, "Cool it! Everybody cool it! Whattaya want, Bolan?"

Bolan yelled back, "You can all go but the lady stays!"

"It's okay, Mr. Wang! Do it! Come on, let's go!"

Smiley yelled something in Chinese. The tall guy with teeth turned surprised eyes on her, then moved stiffly toward the boats. The others followed, walking backward, eyes on Bolan.

Smiley roled into cover in the trees and hissed, "The *papers*, Mack!"

"A moment," he replied quietly.

And a moment was all it took. The Chinese delegation split themselves between the two canoes and moved quickly to the bows as the mainlander crews launched them into the water, then quickly tumbled abroad, many anxious eyes cast into the past rather than toward the future.

But then there was no future; perhaps all knew it.

Bolan held cover behind a tree at the edge of the grove and gave them to the first swell before fingering the little gadget at his belt.

They went together, the two explosions coming as one just as the canoes lifted into the swell. Bolan saw the twin flash and glimpsed hurtling fragments before the outriggers disappeared beyond the wall of water.

Smiley, kneeling beside him, gasped, "My *God!*"

"*Their* God," Bolan murmured.

At next view, both boats were afire and foundering, people were threshing about out there and screaming while beyond the coral reef their pickup vessel was coming about in a fast landward turn.

"They can't get in there," Smiley observed.

"No way," Bolan agreed. He was shedding his weapons. He thrust the chattergun on Smiley and said,

133

"Cover me," then took a running dive toward that pandemonium out there.

The hoods from streetcorner America should have spent more of their time in the Hawaii surf and less in the bars and niteries of Waikiki during their sojourn there; most of them seemed to be spluttering and screaming for help.

The water actually was not all that deep in the flats, but it could be a panic situation for a guy who wasn't familiar with ocean surf.

These were the least of Mack Bolan's worries. He sought a Chinese gentleman who'd last been seen chained to a briefcase—probably a dead one, considering his position in the doomed boat—and he found the guy, half-submerged and drifting landward. Bolan nudged the body on in, tugging at the chain and rolling the guy onto his back in the frothy surf at water's edge.

A wild-eyed Martin Pensa came lunging at Bolan from the flow of a heavy roller, clawing at an empty holster and grunting insane threats. Smiley stepped coolly down from the grove with the chattergun spitting, cutting Pensa down at the knees and flopping him screaming into the foam, then raising the firetrack to chop at two others who'd found standing room close to shore. These promptly disappeared beneath the waves, reappearing cautiously an instant later to paddle toward a landfall farther down the beach.

"Hell with them," Bolan panted. "The chain, Smiley! Cut the chain!"

She did so with a brief burst from the chattergun, then tossed the weapon to Bolan and snatched up the goods.

A police siren was wailing along Kalakaua, very close.

134

"Let's split!" she cried. "There'll be a cop for every tree before long!"

Bolan was catching his breath and looking the other way.

The big yacht was running slowly along the coral reef to the seaward side.

"That's Chung," Bolan said.

"Can't win them all, Slugger," Smiley told him. "Come on!"

"Haven't lost a damn thing yet," Bolan argued. He ran up to the grove, sat down with the AutoMag, steadied himself, and took a cool sighting on the yacht.

Smiley pranced beside him, pleading. "Mack, this is crazy! Let's get *out* of here!"

"Too late already," he said. "Patterson's quick-reaction boys will already be sealing the area. I can't fight those guys."

"Who the hell is Patterson?"

"A new non-enemy. Stand aside, Smiley. Let's give Chung one for the road."

The girl flopped clear. Bolan promptly unleashed Big Thunder, squeezing off twice and pausing for evaluation, then letting go in rapid fire until the clip was empty.

He didn't know what he'd hit, but the effect was apparent. The big boat promptly showed its tail in a quick surge toward open sea.

Bolan muttered, "There you go."

"You're wild, *wild!*" Smiley cried.

Bolan strapped on his gear as he replied to that. "Sure, but with method. That's my only exit. I had to clear it."

"That's nutty! You can't swim out—"

"Who's swimming? I'm going surfing. Ever try it?"

"Sure, but . . ."

"You're a free agent. It's your decision, but it'll have to be a quick one. Stay here and meet the cops or join the party beyond the reefs. What say?"

"What party?"

He pointed to the second boat and handed her the radio. "That one. See if you can raise them while I get the boards."

She said, "Nutty—*nutty!*"

Police sirens were now screaming in from every landward direction.

Bolan jogged down to the surfboard rack and selected a pair, then dodged into the grove and began hurling smoke cannisters.

"Let's move it," he called to the girl. "This won't slow them much, but it'll help."

"Carl's standing by!" she called back exultantly.

Bolan returned to the beach and tossed the boards out.

"Lady's choice," he said, smiling solemnly.

Smiley took a clean run into the surf, the handle of Wang's briefcase clamped between her teeth. Bolan followed, moving expertly onto the board and extending a hand to steady the girl as she boarded hers.

The chemical smokescreen was moving on the wind, filling the groves with dense black clouds and scudding along the beach in both directions.

Mack Bolan and his lady, their barks launched firmly upon the breasts of the water, paddled quietly out to sea, on an angling course toward the head of the coral reef.

The Kuhio beach party, out of time and place, was over.

King Fire, and all that name portended, lay in the immediate future.

18: Showdown Hand

The Honolulu cops were a well-disciplined, professional outfit. In most any other situation, it would have been a genuine pleasure for Harold Brognola to observe their operation. In the present context of personal interest, the observation was almost painful.

These people knew their business.

Patterson was out there somewhere in a chopper, directing the operation from the air. A layered police line had been established along the inland perimeter of the park, with specially equipped tac teams poised for a penetration into the sealed area. Backup units prowled the streets and manned roadblocks on all escape routes. Several helicopters were in the area, and in direct communications with the ground forces.

If that was not enough, Brognola's Line One units were on their way from Schofield Barracks to add their heft to the situation.

Brognola himself was seated in a comfortable armchair at the edge of the communications turret in the tactical center, listening to the radio monitors and building an image in his mind of the scene out there.

The initial problem, the smoke, had dissipated. A pincers movement was closing along the beach from each end, tac teams had penetrated from inland, and choppers were moving continually above the tactical zone in methodical search patterns.

It was a sweet net the guy was weaving.

Meanwhile, hordes of interested spectators had gathered to add a note of complication to the proceedings. Also, several outriggers and a dozen or so youngsters on surfboards were lying just off the beach, dispersing when ordered to do so by PA from one of the choppers, then immediately regrouping and continuing the vigil.

The first sour note, from the police viewpoint, came about ten minutes after the alarm had gone down. The drag line of combat-equipped officers had completed a sweep from inland to the beach sands, without contact.

Brognola slid to the edge of his chair and listened alertly to the radio conversation reporting that event.

Greg Patterson, his gruff voice muffled in the background of helicopter noises, was fit to be tied.

"Go through again!" he ordered. "Beat every bush, move every rock. The guy *couldn't* have slipped through." Then he turned with a fury to his airborne units. "Choppers two and three, extend your patterns by a thousand yards! Chopper four, take another run along those reefs! If you see as much as a floating *stick*, you go down and check it out!"

Brognola lit a cigar and cheerily commented, "Well, well."

A communications technician turned to him with a diffident smile. "I think the guy was gone a minute after the alarm went down," he confided. "I bet the first chopper on the scene could have nailed him—if they'd known what to look for."

"What should they have been looking for?" the fed asked, interested.

138

"A swimmer. Or a surfer."

Out of the mouths of babes. Brognola grinned, remembering several past adventures in which the redoubtable Mack Bolan had evaded the clutch of the law via daring escapes in the sea.

He asked the dispatcher, "Whatever became of that surveillance on the commandeered boat from Ala Wai?"

"That's chopper four's assignment, sir. He was doubling for a few minutes, there, then the lieutenant pulled him into the Bolan hunt exclusively. I guess they can always pick up that boat again. It's just been idling around out there, anyway, standing off Waikiki. That is, last I heard."

"I see. Well, you have an interesting theory concerning Bolan. You should pass that on to the lieutenant."

"Who, me? No, sir, that's not my department. But it's a good theory, I believe. All the guy had to do was strip to his shorts and take off. And even if he didn't strip . . . You know those black tights he wears? You ever see the surfing suits some of these people wear? Get those tights soaking wet, I bet they'd look just like a surf suit."

"Maybe you're in the wrong department," Brognola said soberly.

The technician smiled at the compliment. "Well, I read a lot. And this guy Bolan is a fascinating subject. I've been keeping up on him for a long time."

"This one may be the end of the saga," Brognola replied. He left his chair and went to Patterson's cubicle, picked up the phone, placed a call to Pacific Military Command, and ordered himself a helicopter.

Before he could get out of there, the phone rang

with a call for him, from another office in that same command.

"Justice thirteen four twenty-one, electronic intelligence report," said the caller. "Possible subject contact. A written report is in the file, sir. Would you like to hear the recording?"

"I would," Brognola assured the guy.

"Stand by, sir. The quality is poor. This was monitored on a UHF Citizens Band channel, very weak signal source emanating from the western side of Oahu. It's very brief, sir. Listen closely, please."

A moment later, Brognola heard an excited feminine voice saying, "This is SOG Thirty-two. Is that you out there? Quick, is it you?" An agitated male voice responded: "Smiley, thank God! What the hell is he doing?"

"The usual. I believe we're coming out. Can you assist?"

"You bet. Meet you halfway. Get that guy out of there!"

"On our way."

That was the end of the recording. The intelligence officer inquired, "Did you understand all of it, sir?"

"Yes, but it's a negative," Brognola lied. "Remove it from the file and destroy it."

"It is customary, sir, to—"

"Don't quote customs to me, Lieutenant. I said *remove* and *destroy*. Do you understand me? Destroy it."

"Yes, sir. I understand, sir."

"Hold all further contacts until I call for them. I'll be leaving this location."

The fed hung up and got out of there.

As he passed through the control room, he caught the technician's eye and told him, "Don't close that book yet."

"Sir?"

"The saga of that fascinating subject. There could be many chapters left in the guy."

"Frankly, sir, I hope so."

"So," said the fed, as he stepped outside, "do I."

It was an older inter-island cruiser with a compact cabin, low headroom, and only the minimal comforts of home, but she looked like sheer heaven to Smiley Dublin.

She allowed Tommy Anders to fuss over her and tape Band-Aids over a couple of minor hurts she'd incurred during the wild scramble on Kuhio, then she sank wearily onto the lounge with a sigh and a quiet, "Oh boy."

Bolan and Lyons were topside, searching for silver wings in the sky and plotting a casual course past Diamond Head in the distant wake of the *Pele Phoenix*.

"Isn't that guy something else?" Anders asked her in a quiet voice.

"If you're speaking of Mack the Ripper," Smiley replied wearily, "then that has got to be the understatement of the century."

"What happened back there?"

"Oh, the usual this and that. Blew a couple of boats out of the water. Depleted the criminal population of Hawaii by about one-third. Slew a brace of high-ranking foreign crooks. Made a screaming fool of the Honolulu Police Department. Let's see . . . is that all?"

Anders was chuckling. "Sometimes I just can't believe that guy," he said, believing it nevertheless.

"No—that isn't all. Toss me that briefcase, will you."

Anders picked up the case and set it on the table, fingering the shattered chain and running a hand along

141

the closure. "There's an interesting story here, I'll bet," he said. "You better hope the box is watertight, though."

"Didn't get too wet," she said, smiling. "Carried it in my mouth, like a great she-cat. As for interesting stories, would you believe I shot it off a man's arm?"

Anders clucked his tongue. "Better watch the company you keep, young lady. That guy is contagious."

Smiley shivered at the memory. "That's not all I shot," she murmured. "Somehow, though, it . . . well, it has no meaning. Know what I mean? No meaning."

Gently, Anders told her, "The meaning, maybe, is in that case. Want me to open it?"

She nodded her head. "Please. Do you have a cigarette?"

He lit a Salem and passed it to her, then went to work on the briefcase with a pocket knife.

Smiley smoked with studied deliberation and watched the operation through narrowed eyes.

"Hope it's not booby-trapped," Anders said. "How would I know?"

She gave her head a vague toss and assured him, "It's not. I saw him put the stuff in there."

"Him who?"

"Him who Wang Ho."

"Who the hell is Wang Ho?" Anders asked, laughing delightedly. "This is getting ridiculous, you know. Loon, Chung, Wang chatty bang bang. I never heard such outrageous damn ethnic . . ."

"He's dead. The others, too. And I have the awfullest feeling that . . ."

"What others?"

"Wang's cadre. Those men, Tommy—they were here on deadly serious business."

"Well . . ." Anders was trying to comfort her. "It

142

got them dead, didn't it. And you're seriously alive. Can I tell you, beautiful lady, how very happy we all are that this is true?"

She touched his arm and said, "Thanks, Tom. Tell it to that big bloody bazoom up there, will you? But for him, I'd be a candidate for shark food right now."

"Hey, it *was* a squeaker, eh?"

"In spades. I get so furious every time I think of these damned cops . . ."

"Hey. They have a job, you know. Like us."

"Sure, but why don't they go do it somewhere else? Of all the men to be combing that island for—well, I guess I'll never understand it. Tommy, I think I'm in love with that damn guy."

Anders chuckled as he replied, "Well, join the club. So'm I."

"No, you know, I mean . . ."

"Sure, I know what you mean. Try me instead, kid. I'm a lot safer and my insurance costs less."

"I love you, too, Tommy."

"Yes, I know, you mean . . ."

The girl laughed and kissed his hand. The tightness was leaving her chest. The self-styled wop comic affected her that way—and she was properly grateful. "Do you want me to open that, Tom?"

"I about have it. Here we go . . . ahhh. Your box, ma'am."

She gave him an appreciative bat of the eyes and took possession of the contents of Wang's lockbox. The papers were dry, hardly affected by the moisture of that wild escape from Kuhio.

"That's all wing-wang lingo," the comic observed, peering over her shoulder. "I never could figure out —do you read top to bottom, bottom to top, or kitty-wampus?"

143

Smiley's hands were suddenly shaking. She turned a page, then another.

"Hey, what is it?" Anders inquired excitedly, noting her reaction.

"Get Mack down here, please," she requested in a quivery, barely audible voice.

"Come on, Smiley, dammit! What is it?"

"Would you believe," she said quietly, "another Cuba?"

"What? You mean . . . *missiles?*"

"I don't mean beards!" she said. "Get Mack! Get him down here!"

The man himself appeared in the cabin doorway at that moment, the rugged features set in grim lines.

"A chopper just picked up Chung," he reported. "Toby's on them. But it looks like the end of the trail for me. You guys hang in there. Live large, dammit!"

He was gone again before the startled reaction set in.

Smiley cried, "What's he talking about?"

Anders was scrambling toward the door. He halted there and turned a sick face toward the girl.

He did not need to explain.

The *thump-whump* of 'copter blades directly overhead told the story, loud and clear, and the amplified voice floating down from up there served as mere punctuation to the dismal truth.

"This is the police. You are ordered to lay to, and prepare for boarding."

"Oh God no!" Smiley wailed.

"He won't fight them," Anders said woodenly.

The Executioner had been dealt the showdown hand.

And he could not even call the opener.

19: Fire Line

Two helicopters were hovering in the airspace above the cruiser. The police craft had been joined—no, challenged—by a larger military version and the two were standing off about fifty yards apart, apparently communicating with each other via radio.

It was very obvious to those below that an argument was going on up there, and it continued for several minutes. Then the military craft yielded a bit of airspace and the police job came back to stand directly above the cruiser.

The PA announced: "This is Lieutenant Patterson, Honolulu Police. I'm coming down for a parley. You people down there stay loose."

Lyons waved an acknowledgment.

A door opened up there and a rope ladder slithered out. A large man in a gray suit began slowly descending.

Smiley bumped Carl Lyons with her hip to get his attention and, yelling to make herself heard above the racket from the chopper, told him, "Remember, he's *our* prisoner!"

Lyons gave her a hopeless flash of the eyes and stepped up to give the guy a hand.

Bolan moved to the rail, turned his back to the

whole thing, and consigned his fate to the hands of the universe.

The big guy was standing stiffly on the flying bridge, weapons sheathed, hands casually gripping the rail, the face grim and sort of sad but not belligerent. He wore a skin-tight black outfit with belts running in all directions about that hard torso, supple moccasin-style half-boots on his feet.

Patterson said to him, "So you're the guy."

"I'm the guy."

It was a good voice—clear, vibrant, but not defiant —a trace of New England accent clinging to it.

"You seem to be the center of a jurisdictional dispute. Or so it says here. But I could still take you in, mister. What do you say? Ready to hang it up?"

"I'm always ready. But—thanks, I'll stay."

The cop gestured toward the guy's weapons belt. "Quite an arsenal you carry there. You could have shot me off the ladder. Why didn't you?"

"You're not the enemy," the damned guy told Patterson in that good voice.

"So I've been told." The lieutenant jerked a thumb toward the shore. "Eleven hundred good badges over there, with no cracks showing, say otherwise. You come back to our town, mister, for any reason, and we'll say it to you loud and clear. Understand me?"

"It's a good force, Patterson. Be proud."

"I *am* proud! Who the hell are you to—" The cop caught himself and turned it off, electing to accept it gracefully. "Thanks. I'll take that from one who should know. But it still goes! Don't come back!"

"I'd rather not."

"Keep it that way. What about Oliveras?"

"What about him?"

146

"What does he have that I could use?"

"Plenty. The local infrastructure, the pay-off network, some surprises in your tour industry. Lean on him and he'll break." The damned guy actually grinned at him. "Use my name if you'd like. He fears it more than *omerta*."

Patterson felt his own face cracking in a returning smile. It surprised him. He said, "I'll bet he does, at that. Thanks, I'll remember it. How are your phantoms?"

"My what?"

"The ghosts of past regrets. Don't tell me you don't have them."

"I have them."

"I'll bet."

The cop signaled his chopper for a return. He had studiously ignored those other three down here, the woman and the two other men. Now he looked at the woman and said, "Relax, honey. How's the surf this morning?"

"Splendid," she replied coolly.

Patterson chuckled and reached out for the ladder. One of Brognola's boys steadied it for him. He climbed aboard and turned a final gaze on the big guy at the rail.

"I wash mine down with vodka," he yelled above the rotor racket.

The guy nodded and said something in return, something that was lost in the clatter.

The ninety-nine and 44/100 percent cop did not need to hear it. He knew what the big guy chased his phantoms with.

"Have a bucket on me," he muttered, and went on up the ladder.

The military chopper lifted away and climbed to a holding altitude. Brognola shook hands with the man in black as he advised him, "That's one you owe me, soldier. And don't think it came easy."

"I know the cost," Bolan replied in a solemn voice.

There would be no "thanks" between these two friendly adversaries. Obvious respect was there, and mutual admiration. It was enough.

"As for you people," Brognola said, his gaze flicking toward the other three, "you'd better have some damn hot business going here or we're all going to be behind bars."

Bolan abruptly wheeled about and went below.

Brognola took Smiley by an elbow and steered her in that same direction. "Come along, SOG Thirty-two," he said. "I'm very anxious to hear what you've been doing these past four reportless weeks."

The girl planted her feet and told him, "I'll have to ask you to formally identify yourself, Mr. Brognola."

He said, "Well, I'll be damned."

"I'm serious."

"I can see that." He dug for his wallet and produced the necessary proof.

The girl smiled soberly and said, "We figured you for SOG Control—but who would know, in this nutty business?"

"Nutty, indeed," he agreed. His gaze flicked to Lyons. "Carl? What's happening?"

"Chung is off for Hawaii in a helicopter. Toby's tailing in a chase plane. Bolan flushed the guy and we've been nudging him toward his secret place. Close to paydirt now, we think. We had to team up, Hal. The situation was simply too critical. There was no alternative."

148

"I figured that. You did right. Just don't ever put it in writing."

"Oh hell no."

Smiley's gaze had been alternating rapidly between the two. Her face was now reflecting a dawning revelation. She said, "Thanks for your confidence, guys."

Lyons seemed embarrassed. He said, "Smiley, I . . ."

The chief fed took it onto himself. "The world is full of strange secrets, Miss Dublin. Don't stub your toe on any of them."

"Don't worry, I won't," she replied, and flounced off below.

Brognola sighed. "Do you know?—my wife never believes a thing I tell her. I wonder why."

Lyons suggested, "Let's go below, Hal. I'll update you."

"Somebody better run the boat," Anders said, over a handshake with Brognola. "Go ahead. I signed for it, I'll swing for it."

The comic remained on the bridge while the other two joined Bolan and the lady in the cabin.

The big guy was seated at the mess table, staring perplexedly at Smiley's Chinese papers.

Brognola inquired, "What the hell is this?"

"One of those strange secrets," the girl replied. "Watch your toes, boss."

"Come on, knock it off," he said irritably. "What is it?"

"Try World War Three," she groused.

"I hope you're not serious."

"Fifty-fifty serious, anyway. According to this top document, the man who was wearing it on a wrist manacle is high in the party hierarchy. He—"

"Wang Ho," Brognola said quietly.

Smiley flared, "So what the hell do you need with me!"

"Hey, now—"

"Hey *hell!* Do you know where I've *been* these four reportless weeks?"

"Look, if an apology will help, you've got it. I'm sorry. It's a paranoid business. I can't help that. Nobody's underrating your value *or* your contributions. I'm tired, cranky, and suffering jet lag. I just mortgaged my office to that Goddamned cop up there. And, to top it all, I'm so damned thrilled to see you all alive and well . . ." The chief fed paused and swiped at his eyes. "Aw, fuck it," he muttered.

Smiley was crying. She put her arms about his neck and kissed him.

"I'm a dope," she said. "Forgive me."

Brognola's face was several shades of crimson. He patted her bare back and said something gruff and unintelligible.

It could be an emotional business as well as paranoid.

Smiley stepped into the galley and wet her face from the water spigot.

Bolan snared a wrinkled cigarette pack and quietly lit one.

Lyons said to Brognola, "I guess you got my report."

The chief nodded and cast a reflective gaze toward the girl. "Wang was a lucky guess," he told her. "Carl's report reached me on the plane, coming across this morning. Or whenever that was. God, it seems ages. Anyway, I simply added the pieces together. Our China watchers have been wondering for some time about the connection between Wang and General

Loon. When I got the make on Chung—well, it was just two and two."

"Wang is dead," Bolan quietly advised him.

"Oh. Damn. I hope you burned the body."

"I'm afraid not."

"Doesn't matter," Smiley put in. "He left us his coffin." Her eyes flicked to the papers on the table. "One of those documents is a deployment order."

"Deployment of what?" Brognola asked.

"Missiles."

That one startled him. He said, "Hell, they don't have—*tactical* missiles?"

"Strategic," she said. "Intermediate Range Ballistic Missiles."

That one froze him.

He shuffled the documents together and placed them in the briefcase. "This is a lock-up," he declared, all warmth gone from that voice now. "You'll play the three monkeys routine." The official gaze fell on Bolan. "Make that *four* monkeys. The fourth *sits* on his hands."

Bolan said, just as coldly, "If I was a monkey, maybe that's what I'd do. But I'm not, and I can't."

"The *hell* you can't!"

Bolan was not arguing the point. He was simply laying it out. "It's too late for that, Hal. The guy's running toward his toys right now. You've got the best tracker in your stable on his tail. She'll run the guy to where the marbles are. And this could be the only chance to pick them up. This is not a problem in international diplomacy. It's not an act of aggression by a foreign power. It's simply—"

"That's for someone else to decide!"

"There's no time for someone else."

"I still think . . ."

151

"Okay, lay it out. Would the official Chinese government sponsor something as wild as this? Against the strongest nuclear power in the world? The PRC's don't have more than twenty-five or thirty IRBM's in their whole arsenal. They have no air force, no navy, no strategic strike capability whatever. Balance that against our arsenal. More than a thousand ICBM's that can go wherever we want to send them. Half that many strategic bombers with nukes. Maybe a hundred attack submarines, also with nukes. A fantastic fleet. World War Three, Hal? No way. Not from here, not with a few lousy IRBM's planted at our back gate. Their best range is three thousand miles."

"I have to go with Mack," Lyons said.

"Me, too," from Smiley. "Except . . . knowing the Chinese mind as I *think* I do . . . they wouldn't back down much if we started rattling weapons at them. And that's what worries me. I keep remembering how close we came to nuclear war with the Russians over Cuba."

"China is not technically classified as a nuclear power," Brognola mused. "Not yet."

"So why an insane deployment of what little they have?" Lyons wondered.

"That's what I keep saying," Bolan told them. "This is not an official act of the Chinese government."

"Who signed this deployment order?" Brognola asked the girl.

"Loon Chuk Wan. Countersigned by Wang."

Bolan was probing her eyes. "What was it you were telling me . . . something Wang said, about the papers . . . you said it translated to—"

"This is where the body is buried."

Brognola asked, "Whose body?"

152

"It's a figure of speech," Smiley explained.

"This is very messed up," Lyons said. "How does the mob fit into all this?"

"Maybe not at all," Bolan quietly decided. "And maybe all the way. We'll have to sift that out later. The boys could be simply patsies. They've been ripe for something like this, with their own crazy schemes for the Big Thing. I'm reading it as a con job until I have something more definite to read."

Brognola asked, "You're saying the commission doesn't *know* these guys are bringing in missiles over here?"

Bolan nodded. "Or else they've been led to believe that they are defensive emplacements."

"That's possible, I guess. Or maybe it's a double con. You know how the boys operate. They'll let them bring in the stuff, then they knock it over for their own uses."

Lyons said, "Okay, let's play with that for a minute. How could the boys make use of IRBM emplacements?"

"I could give you a couple uses right off the bat," Brognola said. "In two words: blackmail and extortion."

"On an international scale," Lyons added. "It could fit with their Big Thing."

"It could," Bolan agreed. "But right now, the power here is Chung. The question is: is he acting as a Chinese general or as a mob enforcer."

"Can you answer the question?" Brognola asked him.

"No. Except last night, outside his stronghold, he was talking to this guy Wang. They were enjoying some private joke. Chung said something about beheading ten thousand Italians."

Brognola threw up his hands and declared, "Hell, it gets worse and worse instead of better and better. I *have* to lock it up!"

Bolan said, "Consider this first. There's a concealed missile site somewhere in these islands. We've identified them as IRBM's, which gives them a striking range of three thousand miles. Regardless of *who* intends to use them, the fact remains that they are there for *use*. Point?"

"Point," Brognola agreed. "Go ahead."

"We're all agreed that it's a nutty scheme. So isn't that what the thinking heads of the world are trembling in their dreams about these days?—nutty schemes from faulty thinkers that could launch the whole world into nuclear holocaust?"

"Point. Keep going."

"Take the best case. The mob owns the missiles. They plan to use them, in one mad scheme or another. Can we take any comfort in that?"

"None at all. Go to the worst case."

"*Chung* owns the missiles. Not the Chinese government. Chung. For some mad scheme of *his* own. Comfort?"

"Christ no," Brognola said, shivering.

"Suppose," Bolan mused, "a renegade Chinese general wanted to embarrass the hell out of somebody back home. Suppose he couldn't stomach all these recent wavings of olive branches and talk of detente. Maybe he even *fears* it, in a paranoid sense. Suppose this same guy knew how to smuggle a few of his country's precious missiles to a secret site within range of his would-be enemies. Then suppose he sat back and lofted one into San Francisco, one or two into Los Angeles, maybe one into Seattle or Portland or San Diego—with nuclear warheads aboard. That

154

would sure as hell mark the end of detente, wouldn't it?"

"To say the least," Lyons quietly agreed.

"It would take a madman," Brognola growled.

"That's right," Bolan said. "Do you have a recent psychiatrist's report on General Loon Chuk Wan—or on Secretary Wang Ho?"

"Goddammit!" Brognola said, and repeated it.

"What does it take to launch these IRBM's?" Lyons wanted to know.

"It's a sophisticated system," Bolan assured him. "But if they can bring the birds in and plant them, they sure as hell can bring in the technicians to fly them."

"It comes down to this, doesn't it," said Lyons, "—*intent.*"

Bolan nodded. "Add that to present circumstances —which are probably at this moment *panic.* We've been leaning on the guy, hard, deliberately hoping to find his button. If I'd known it was a nuclear one . . ."

"That's what I mean," Brognola said. "It's no game for amateurs."

"What is a pro, Hal?" Bolan asked him.

"Hell, they're . . ."

"People like you and me," Bolan agreed. "Sitting off the firing line, pushing options into a cocked hat and fishing for them blindfolded. Okay." His gaze swung to Smiley Dublin. "We've asked everybody but the right body about this problem. You lived with the guy for a month, Smiley. You've warmed his bed and shared his food. You know his language and probably his nightmares. You've read his mail and—I wouldn't be surprised—his diary. What's the guy up to?"

"I've been telling you," she said quietly. "World

155

War Three. His version, anyway. The general is a fanatic hawk, like most of the others in the military over there. Father Mao is in his eighties—he's sick—he's dying and he knows it. He's trying to handpick his own successor, and the hawks know *that*. The general staff has become very standoffish. They're lining up factions in the struggle for power—and they're winning. But Mao is still the power—will be until he dies. The generals all know that. They're scared to death he's going to sell them out, just to strengthen his own hand. They don't give a whooping damn for the so-called revolution. Politics, for them, is simply the means to an end. And it doesn't take a China expert to tell you that hawks do not thrive on a diet for doves."

"Out of the mouths of babes," Brognola said quietly.

"Thanks," she said, "but I'm no babe. Mack said it. I'm a pro."

"You are that," Brognola conceded.

"What about Chung the man?" Bolan asked her. "How do you read him? Right now?"

"Right now?—you've said that, too. He's running scared."

Bolan said to Brognola, "You can't lock me up, Hal. You can shoot me, but you cannot lock me up."

The man with the NSC mandate had arrived at his decision. He said, the voice barely audible, "We'll play both games. I'll get this stuff into Pacific Command and set up a roundtable. You people forget that you saw me today. I wasn't even here."

"We may need your chopper," Bolan told him. "And if we find the joint, we may need more than that."

"I'll send the chopper back. And I'll send you what-

156

ever else I can, as you ask for it. But for God's sake test the water before you leap in."

"Pele water," Bolan murmured.

"Huh?"

"No need to test. The temperature out there is pre-ordained. It's the hellgrounds, Hal."

The chief fed shook hands all around, went to the doorway, then turned back with a weary smile. "So what's new?" he asked the hellbenders.

20: Infinite Zero

Brognola was true to his word, but it was a different bird that returned for them. This one was a fully armed and crewed UH-1 D "Huey" gunship—pilot, copilot, two gunners—with plenty of troop space.

A fifth man descended to take custody of the cruiser and return her to Ala Wai.

The pilot was Chief Warrant Steve Richards, an army veteran with many Vietnam missions under his belt, a no-nonsense guy who had apparently already been sketchily briefed on this present peace-time mission.

Brognola also sent a care package for the airborne commandos—maps, a xeroxed profile sheet of known Chinese weaponry, jungle survival kits, a miscellany of tools, gadgets, and weapons, and a change of clothes for Smiley Dublin—OD pants, shirt, jacket, cap, boots.

Skipper Richards asked for "Stryker," shook hands, and told him, "My orders are to *take* orders, *any* orders—from you." The guy was looking Bolan up and down as he said this, and it was obvious that he knew the name was not Stryker.

Bolan placed Smiley with her new clothing in the copilot's seat and assigned her the task of developing communications with the chase plane. Anders was put to work collating the stuff from the care package and putting together combat sets. Bolan and Lyons sat down with the maps and intelligence data, Bolan concentrating on Chinese missile developments while Lyons studied terrain conditions on Hawaii.

The copilot brought back headsets with radio and intercom hook-ups.

The gunners were checking and arming their weapons.

Lyons, looking around with admiration, commented, "This is a hell of a fire platform."

"Beats the old 1 B's," Bolan agreed. He was studying the profile sheet of a Chinese missile. "New wrinkle here, too."

"What is that?"

"Looks like the PRC's have a mobile IRBM."

"Mobile?"

"Yeah. Can be mounted on wheels or rails. Similar to the Russian SS-XZ Scrooge."

"What's the range?" Lyons wondered.

"About equal to the Polaris A3, says here. That's 2,880 miles. Packs a warhead of one megaton."

Lyons whistled softly through his teeth. "You were right. They could pop them right into L.A."

Lyons had a family in Los Angeles.

Bolan said, "Not if we don't allow it."

"Do we actually *know* that they have those things?"

"I guess. This sheet isn't even marked secret." He glanced forward and saw that Smiley and the skipper were hitting it off. He poked the intercom button and asked, "Any contact, Smiley?"

"No contact. I'm afraid she's out of range."

Richards advised, "Better reception up top if you want to lose the time for the climb."

"Let's do it," Bolan replied.

"Right. Here we go."

"I'm worried about her fuel range," Lyons fretted. "She can't fly circles forever."

"Probably riding high on them," Bolan guessed. "Try to keep the sun behind her. And you're right. She's flying two or three miles to their one."

"That's what I mean. She could fly dry."

"Toby's a good pilot," Bolan said. "The worst is yet to come. If those guys drop low across the island, it could be nip and tuck. You could lose a whole squadron of choppers in those mountains."

The two lost themselves in quiet thought.

A moment later, the pilot advised, "I believe your lady is getting a contact. Punch in channel three."

Bolan made the switch in time to hear Toby Ranger's faint voice reporting. " . . . to death about you. Is everyone okay?"

"Fat and sassy," Smiley's jubilant tones boomed. "We're airborne, forty minutes to your rear. What's your situation?"

"Normal," came the faint reply. "Some navigator this guy is. Island hopping. We've overflown Molokai and the northwest tip of Maui. Now running the Kealaikahiki Channel due west, about ten miles south of Lanai."

Lyons was furiously running a plot line on the chart.

"Roger," said Smiley. "Stand by. I believe the man wants in."

Bolan radioed, "Good show, Toby. What's your fuel situation?"

"Hi, Captain Thunder. Caught your fireworks display back here. You ever think about social security?"

"All the time. Fuel report, please."

"I have enough, unless this guy wants to touch every landfall in the damned ocean."

"It's a break for us, Toby. Maybe we can play

160

catch-up. Play it cool, don't spook them. The game has changed. It's gone terminal."

"Oh, wow. Okay. Is the gang all here?"

"Gang's all here, right. Meet you at the picnic. Keep us advised, but let's also keep it radio minimal."

"Right. See you at the games, James."

Bolan chuckled solemnly and switched back to intercom. "Skipper, set a dead course for Mauna Loa, and let's highball it all we can."

"Wilco. You ready to tell me what we're doing?"

"Hunt and Kill, Skipper."

"Aha! Uh, I was at 'Nam about the same time you were. Flew some missions with the Pen Teams. Which one did you have?"

Yeah, sure, the guy knew.

Bolan replied, "Able Team."

"Ah. Yeah. Well, it's oldtimesville, isn't it. You going to give me a fire assignment?"

"I hope so, Skipper."

Yes, Bolan hoped so. The big UH-1 D gunships carried impressive armament, including several machine guns, twenty-millimeter cannon, and a pod of eighteen 2.75 rockets. Bolan had tremendous respect for their firepower; he would most likely need everything the Huey could deliver.

Bolan's thoughts drifted, recalling the invaluable role of the big birds in Vietnam. Such a shame, also, that the military excellence of that age should have become so eclipsed by the nation's thunderous revulsion for the war itself. Nobody liked wars—especially the guys fighting them. But there was such a thing as pride. Mack Bolan was proud of the military excellence displayed in Vietnam. Those Hueys, now. There had been times when he had seen as many as seventy-five of them swooping in simultaneously to disgorge troops

161

in an area no larger than a football field—marveling that they could get in and out without collision. Guys like Richards had guts of iron and the steady hand of a brain surgeon. Once, his team encircled in an impenetrable, enemy-held rain forest, Bolan had been rescued by one of the big birds. She'd come in to hover above the treetops, guns spitting defiance in all directions, dropped her lifelines through the trees, and lifted that trapped team out of there as smoothly as an eagle snatching field mice.

Yes. Mack Bolan could take pride in human excellence—whatever the situation.

And, yeah, Richards. Oldtimesville. Time had a way of circling back on a guy. Infinite zero.

He hoped that Chief Warrant Steve Richards had not lost the sharply honed cutting edge of human excellence that was developed in Vietnam; it would be needed, here, now.

Other thoughts crowed his mind during the time of relaxation before the storm. Carl Lyons, there. What a guy. Human excellence? Damn right. Very human, too. Not like Bolan, not a walking dead man. A wife and kid in L.A. How did he square his responsibilities to them with this weird life he had chosen? Or had it chosen him? Lyons hadn't been exactly honest with Bolan. Which was okay. As Brognola said, it was a paranoid business. What about Carl's professed naivete with regard to the Mafia-China angle? Paranoia? On a near-deathbed in Vegas, the guy had told Bolan that he was chasing a Chinese connection. An L.A. cop? Chasing ChiComs? Early on here in Hawaii, he'd poo-poohed a Mafia-China alliance. How long had Carl Lyons actually been chasing the Chinese connection?

And Smiley Dublin—now there was a study. *Female*

excellence—no matter how you turned it. Was it mere coincidence that a talented showgirl turned under-cover fed was also an accomplished linguist—and, no less, a China expert? How did these people come to-gether? Infinite zero? Maybe.

The hottest comic, ethnician Tommy Anders: now there was a case for wonderment. How long before Vegas, actually, had he been playing Brognola's wild games? He'd told Bolan back then that the mob had been laying on him for refusing to play their games on the night-club circuit. True or false? Probably false. So what led a national personality like this guy into the cloak-and-dagger game? Infinite zero, sure.

Toby Ranger—mouth of solid brass and heart of gold, not to mention those delightful other dimensions. She could fly anything with wings, could outshoot the average cop, had the courage of a lioness with cubs. Where the hell had she hatched from? From infinite zero?

Lyons broke into Bolan's introspections with pithy summation. "This one could be for all the marbles."

Bolan smiled wearily and replied, "Watch the store, Carl. I've got to crash. Eyes haven't closed for two days and nights."

It was like turning a switch, that transition from alert wakefulness to restorative slumber. It was another trick he had learned in the death jungles of Vietnam—"combat sleep"—eyes and ears half open and alert to any suggestion of peril, the thinking mind at rest and gathering strength for the trials that lay ahead.

He did not even hear his friend's reply, so it must have been an assent. And he had no awareness of the routine events of that flight, no sense of time passing. He was, however, jolted back by the faint, distressed voice of Toby Ranger deep in the earphones.

163

"I can't believe it! They just disappeared—right over the crater! Going down for a closer look!"

Smiley cautioned, "Be careful."

Bolan asked Lyons, "What is it? Where are they?"

"Sounds like the home stand."

Bolan punched his button to tell Toby, "Get a marker down and get away from there!"

"You don't understand," came the faint reply. "One second they were there and the next second they weren't. They simply disappeared, *zot!* I'm on it now. It's a—uh oh, ground fire! *I'm hit!*"

He waited a moment for further word, then prodded for it. "Toby! How bad?"

There was no response.

Smiley screamed it, rattling Bolan's phones: "Toby! *Toby!*"

Lyons groaned, "My God."

Richards reported, "I had her on radar, Stryker. She blipped out. She's down."

"Do you have a position fix?"

"Affirm. Twenty minutes out. And that's mighty rough country down there."

Twenty minutes.

For those living on the heartbeat, that could be an infinity of eternities.

And for Mack Bolan, especially, it was a circle-back to nowhere . . . to infinite zero.

21: King Fire

The *X* on the skipper's chart marked a chaotic jumble of rock outcroppings—great hollow depressions with jagged sides rising to imposing ridges, and all interlaced with seemingly impenetrabale jungle growth—wild country for sure, the legacy of the violence which accompanied the birth of this volcanic island.

Smiley shuddered. "Oh! If she's down in there . . ."

Bolan touched the skipper's shoulder. "I just saw a flash of something at two o'clock—there it is again!"

"Right, I have it."

"That's it!" Anders cried.

That was it, all right—the crumpled wreckage of a small plane, perched near the top of a steep slope and all but hidden in dense vegetation.

"Recent crash," the pilot judged. "Otherwise the jungle would have covered it over."

They were almost directly above the spot now. Bolan said, "It's a bad angle, isn't it?"

"We can lower you in, if you're game."

Bolan was. He went to the waist and got into the personnel rig.

A moment later, he was swinging free and descending into the trees. He was on the ground for just a few minutes, and his face, when it reappeared at the personnel door, held a mixture of defeat and hope. The crewmen pulled him aboard and he reported to the anxious team: "I don't know how she could have survived that, but maybe she did. Bit of blood in the cockpit, that's all. Someone took her out. Vehicle tracks nearby, I'd say a jeep or some sort of ATV. Steel mesh fence about fifty yards from the impact point—can't even see it from up here. The sign says Pan Pacific Geological Laboratory. It also says to keep the hell out. I didn't like the feel of it. I think it's pay-dirt."

Smiley was biting her knuckles. She said, "God, Mack. If she's . . ."

"No, wait," Lyons said, rubbing his forehead in concentration. "We checked that place out two weeks ago. It's a scientific research group, doing volcano studies."

"Were you in there?" Bolan asked him.

"No. But we ran a paper check. They're even partially funded through a U.S. grant. It checked out solid. Uh . . . tectonic studies."

"What's that?"

"Beats me. Something to do with geological evolution, formation of earth layers, something like that. They have an extinct crater back in there somewhere and—*wait* a minute!"

"Right—Toby said the chopper disappeared *over a crater.*"

Smiley said, "Well, you wouldn't expect them to put up a sign saying *missile site,* would you? What the hell?—cover groups are a dime a dozen. Let's go take a look."

Anders was working another line of thought. "Pele Phoenix," he said. "Fits like a hand in a glove. From the ashes of an old fire, a new one arises."

166

"And rises and rises," Smiley added. "Clear to California."

"Sure. That's *got* to be it."

"What a beautiful cover," the girl said. "Who would think to look for a missile base in a volcano!"

"What do you think?" Lyons asked Bolan.

"King Fire," Bolan said. "And, sure, it fits. Nobody would question the movement of heavy equipment into a place like that. And it's not unusual for scientific installations to be fenced off and guarded against trespassers."

"What trespassers?" Anders commented, shivering slightly. "Mountain goats, maybe."

"Cute time is over," Bolan decided. "Let's go look it over, Skipper. Look right down their throats. If we draw so much as revolver fire, you've got yourself a fire mission."

"Rah-jer. Here we go. Gunners, take stations."

Smiley was evicted from her seat as the copilot slid in to man his station.

They came in at treetop level, breaking into a clearing several hundred feet beyond the fencing. At dead center was a prefabricated building, long and flat and practically invisible, poised at the rim of a shallow depression which from on high would look like a crater. At this altitude, it was apparent that a huge tarpaulin, painted the same color as the surrounding lava rock, was suspended like a bowl into the depression.

Beneath that tarp, sure, could be a genuine crater—with a surface diameter of about 100 feet. That was small, as Hawaiian craters go. The giant Haleakala Crater on Maui could swallow the island of Manhattan. This one, if indeed it were a crater, could certainly swallow a few illicit ballistic missiles.

167

The cincher was standing nearby on glistening rails, concealed in covering vegetation—a small gantry crane.

Bolan said, "Bingo. Lift away, Skipper."

Two men in shirtsleeves had stepped out of the building and were looking up at the chopper, hands on hips, simply watching. One of them waved genially as the Huey pulled away.

Smiley's breath caught in her throat. "That's Nate Flora," she exclaimed.

"Where's the helicopter?" Lyons wondered.

"Maybe it flew under the tarp," Lyons said.

The Huey was now circling and climbing to a holding altitude, several hundred yards beyond the installation.

Bolan moved his team to the waist, where they began rigging for combat.

"Here's the way we go," he told them. "It'll have to be a punch-in, ramming all the way, quick-quick numbers. Worse, we'll have to play the ear. Smiley, you stay close on me. I might need your linguistics."

The pilot had joined the clutch for the combat order. The guy's face was sober and a bit drawn, but there was a gleam in the eyes.

"Lyons and Anders will cover our butts outside. Keep that yard clean. Work with Richards here, he can give you plenty of comfort. We'll look for Toby first, and try to spring her. Richards—you see a beautiful blonde staggering around out there, go get her. Carl—if you get clear, try to drop that tarp."

The pilot was passing out radios. He said, "Don't dwell on formalities. You want a blast somewhere, just scream it. Try to give me some sort of coordinates, though. Sarge—you want to tell me now what's under that tarp?"

168

Bolan slung a chattergun from his shoulder and told the guy, "Maybe five or six megatons of hell on earth, Skipper. Don't put any rockets in there. We could have this whole damn island spewing again."

The guy's face turned a bit gray. He said, "What the hell is it?"

"We think it's ChiCom IRBM's. Tell your gunners to play their fire accordingly. Look, give us a standard infantry drop, then pull back for fire support. This is an ear play, so you'll have to use yours, too."

"Right. Are we ready?"

"We're ready."

The pilot returned to his station.

Bolan showed his people a solemn smile. "Live large," he said. "Follow my lead out of here. He'll bring her down to a few feet off the ground. You'll feel the nose dip. That's *go* time. Don't hesitate and don't look back. Hit the ground running and ready for a fight. Any questions?"

"Yeah," the comic-fed said, his face cast in pained lines. "How do you get out of this chicken outfit?"

"You die," Bolan replied with a wry smile.

"I guess I'll stay."

The Huey went in on a descending curve, skimming the treetops and dropping steadily. She broke the clearing and gave a momentary, gut-grabbing upward lurch, then bored on in with the nose high and running parallel to the ground. People were spilling out of that building over there and a siren was sounding when the ship gave the telltale shiver, hanging suspended in a split-second hover, the nose dipping.

Bolan yelled "Tally ho" and launched himself into the jarring descent. The others spilled out behind him and the Huey lifted away, machine guns spitting a withering fire across those grounds in advance of the landing team.

Bolan's piece was blazing before his conscious mind pulled the trigger, and he was aware of chattering hand guns behind him.

On the forward track, a very impersonal thing was happening—men were dying with grotesque screams choking their throats, bodies rolling across the hell-grounds and pumping blood onto the lava rock into pools that could not be absorbed.

He hit the door of the building at full gallop and crashed in, a fresh clip in the chattergun and death on his mind. A trio of khaki-clad Orientals rose up from somewhere and promptly descended into nowhere as death chattered on.

Smiley Dublin ran into his corner vision, a wreath of fire encircling the snout of her weapon—and that part of his mind, mostly submerged now, that gives rise to intellectual activity was sharply jolted by the death snarl on that pretty face.

There were no inner walls here and no back wall whatever, only a gaping wound in what had once been volcanic rock, an elevator shaft which could transport several automobiles at once. The building was crammed with work tables and exotic machinery and, off to one end, a glass cubicle outfitted for lounging during leisure moments.

A pair of familiar Caucasians from Manhattan had just run into there, Dominick and Flora—and, sure, they had to know—there was no China con game here —*La Commissione* were present, alive, and trying to stay well in King Fire—and Bolan was sickened by the stench of depravity represented by all this.

Before he could react, Smiley Dublin was on them,

with her kill mask intact and her gun blowing death into that glass house.

The cubicle walls shattered and the glass rained down in tinkling accompaniment to the shrilling siren, chattering weapons, and the despairing moans of souls departing under duress.

Bolan yelled, "Smiley, hold it!—*hold it!*"

Her weapon fell and she turned to him like a sleep-walker just jolted awake. The voice was small and unbelieving as she cried, "My God, Mack! I was *en-joy-ing* it!"

"That's just gut talk!" he barked. "Toby's in there. Get her out!"

Bolan ran on, to the edge of the pit. Beyond and to his right, behind another glass wall, were consoles and the usual trappings of a launch control center. He spewed that wall with steel-jacket slugs—and they merely bounced off. He pivoted and ran along the rim, found a steel circular stairway, and descended into the pit. Abruptly, all the lights went out and the siren failed and all sounds of gunfire topside dwindled away.

He was in stygian blackness and descending deeper into it when something fluttered high overhead and bright sunlight converted the depths of hell into a twentieth-century nightmare. Gleaming steel casings glittered hotly under the sun and spoke to him of man-made suns that hurtled through the skies in search of mass souls—and, yeah, even here, in this madness, could be found a sort of perverted pride in the ac-complishment of a living species who had climbed down from the trees many, many eons *after* Pele's fires had raged in this pit. An example of human excel-lence, yes—but an excellence run amok.

A pair of them stood there, graceful and threatening yet impotent, incomplete. There were no nose cones—

no payloads. The man who had walked through several hells to reach this place had to stifle an impulse to sit down and laugh, to light a cigarette and hurl taunts at the unfanged wonders from across the world.

He went deeper, into the very bowels of the place, following the sounds of moving feet and hushed voices, and found more unfanged marvels, lying on their sides, asleep and strapped to their beds. And there were tunnels down here, narrow-gauge rails, holes in the rock leading God knew where, and running feet scurrying everywhere.

And there was Chung.

He stood beside a sleeping giant, one hand raised as though to caress it, staring at the man in black with inscrutable eyes.

The Big One told him, "Here's my head, General. Come and take it."

"You did not beat me," the guy said. *"She* beat me."

"Beat is beat," Bolan told him. "Let's go."

"She intercepted the payloads. *She* sent them back. The lotus blossom is my Achilles heels. Is it true?"

Bolan told him, "I guess it is."

The guy turned around and walked away. Bolan called out, then sent a burst of fire around his feet, and the guy walked on.

Pele beat you, guy. I met her, upstairs, just a minute ago.

Bolan let him go, to meet defeat in his own way.

When he returned to the upper level, Carl Lyons was moving gingerly through the litter of dead and dying—looking for faces, probably, that could merit a written report.

"Let's get out of here," Bolan told him.

"What is—did you find—?"

Bolan grabbed his arm and pulled him along. "I

found. There's only one way to finish this place. Let's go."

"Smiley said—"

"Pele."

"Huh?"

"I found her, too."

"Are you okay?"

"I will be—when this place is buried."

The girls were aboard the Huey. It stood there, hovering a few feet above the ground, proud sign and symbol of controlled excellence. Anders ran to join them and they climbed aboard. Bolan went immediately to the command chair and told the excellent human being there: "Take her up. Rocket range. Bury it."

The guy's face drained and he said, "Six megatons worth?"

"A Chinaman's pride worth," Bolan corrected him. "There's nothing down there but rocket fuel. Bury it."

A minute or so later, a succession of bright, streaking arrows of fire whizzed through the Hawaiian skies to enter a primeval hole in the ground.

The hole belched back with rolling flames and towering smoke, a drumbeat succession of thundering, trumpeting explosions that quivered the ground and shook the atmosphere.

Bolan stood in the open doorway of the gunship to watch a mad dream expire and to comfort a weeping lotus blossom who, for one mad moment, had found exultation in violence.

Flames roared into the sky and—for one mad moment of his own—Mack Bolan thought that he saw Mother Pele dancing in the open pit, smiling at him with the face of a lotus blossom.

The one beside him said, "Mack . . . it *is* a paranoid

173

business. I haven't told you everything. Maybe I never can. There *are* many secret games. And I—I . . ."

He said, "Shush. It's okay."

There was nothing so paranoid about an undercover fed who sang and danced, spoke in many tongues and loved in the line of duty—and completely broke a renegade Chinese general.

"How's Toby?" he asked her.

"Hurting, but healthy."

"How's Smiley?"

"Healthy, but hurting. Mack . . . What happened to me down there?"

"Happens to all of us," he told her. "Sooner or later . . . if we're really alive. You found infinite zero. You roared back, Smiley. That's all."

Yeah. Primeval forces were still at work on Planet Earth.

And some of us, thank God, roared back.

Epilogue

The government was a machine, sure, but the machinery was maintained and the program buttons pushed by people. Brognola had exercised a prerogative of his office. He would do it again, whenever he thought that his government would be best served through such an exercise.

He told the big, damned guy, "I'm assuring you safe conduct back to the mainland. Miss Dublin will go along to make sure it doesn't get violated. Soon as she releases you, you're on your own again."

The big guy showed him one of those humorless smiles as he turned the offer back. "Thanks, I'll find my own way back."

"Look," Brognola fumed, "I hocked my soul to spring you out of here. You owe me. Another scrape with the law in this jurisdiction and I'll be hanging by my thumbs from the Washington Monument. I mean to *escort* you back to—"

"No way," the blitzer said adamantly. "If it will make you feel better, though, Smiley can tag along with me. Part of the way, at least."

The chief fed had to settle for that.

Miss Dublin seemed delighted to settle for that.

So it was the end of another wild one. Lyons and Anders would be pushing off soon for Hong Kong, even hotter now on the scent of the Chinese connection.

Toby Ranger would spend a few days in the hospital under medical observation, just to make certain that there were no hidden injuries from that plane crash. Then she would drift toward the Far East.

Smiley would be heading that way, also, as soon as her escort assignment was concluded.

As for the chief fed, it was back to Heat Town—and a lot of explaining to the men in the hotter seats back there.

There were times when Brognola wished he could drift away to the next battle line. It could be difficult enough wearing *one* hat in the rarified higher atmospheres of official Washington—Hal Brognola was trying to juggle two of them, one for the Justice Department and another for the National Security Council.

Sensitive Operations indeed—what a hell of a misnomer.

It had been tough enough trying to overcome a domestic enemy with infinite tentacles trying to eat the country from within. Since it had started sprouting infinite heads, as well—with many of those heads situated outside the country—the task had become next to impossible.

It was a tough world.

Thank God for people like Anders and Lyons, Ranger and Dublin—with a special prayer for the one and only Mack Bolan.

Some kind of guy.

This guy was more than a mere hell *bender*. He ran the place. And there weren't many secrets around this guy.

"How many hats are you wearing these days?" he'd

ask the chief fed, with one of those knowing smiles.

He knew; sure he knew. Probably knew all about the double-agent role for Smiley Dublin—maybe knew, even, about the sensitive mutual assistance operation between the two governments. Or, at least, sensed it.

"I'll get your China gal back to you in a few days," the big guy assured Brognola over that parting hand-clasp.

There was nothing to be gained by playing dumb—except maybe to save a bit of face. Hal Brognola had given away his face long ago. "Do that," he replied. "We couldn't SOG it without her."

"Neither could I," Bolan replied, grinning.

And then, with a spin of the foot, he was gone.

It was a lot of bullshit, of course—a concession to Hal Brognola's missing face. The guy could get along without anybody. He'd been doing it for a hell of a long time. Couldn't last forever, of course. The guy was damned—and, sure, he knew it. Only a doomed man could do the job this guy was doing.

As Brognola watched the big one stride away, he felt a surge of pride. There went one hell of a man—one *excellent* hell of a man!

The chief fed felt dignified—perhaps even consecrated—as he watched the hellbender and the "China gal" fade into the blood-red horizon of a Hawaiian sunset.

"Over the hill and far away," the fed muttered to himself, ". . . and on to the next hellground. Stay hard, guy, dammit. Stay as hard as you are!"

EXECUTIONER 19: DETROIT DEATHWATCH by
DON PENDLETON

Bolan wanted that fortress of Mafia power. He meant to level
the joint, reduce it to rubble, show them what real warfare
could be, get them running scared until they were falling all
over each other and bringing their own individual houses
down in the panic. He wanted to see shockwaves travelling
the entire length of this Detroit-based empire, which stretched
around the world in every direction, and into every country
on the globe – an empire that controlled industries, international banks, multi-national corporations, and even the
policies of small nations. This Detroit mob was a festering
sore in every vital organ of mankind.

So Bolan turned to Detroit with a determined sigh. Judgement had come to the *Ville d'Etroit* – the City of the Strait . . .

0 552 10102 8 – 50p

EXECUTIONER 20: NEW ORLEANS KNOCKOUT by
DON PENDLETON

Marco Vannaducci, the ageing local don in New Orleans, was
dying slowly . . . hounded by the feds. Marco was a desperate
man, trying to hold together his tottering empire – an empire
with annual revenues of around a cool billion. And a dozen
powerful Mafia families up and down the country were waiting for the green light to get together and slice up the action.
. . . Bolan had his timing right. He arrived in town for
Mardi Gras . . . when a combined invasion of New York and
St Louis mobs had also booked seats for the show. The
underworld went berserk. . . .

0 552 10179 6 – 45p

THE DESTROYER: ACID ROCK by RICHARD SAPIR and WARREN MURPHY

Vickie Stoner was a fully-fledged groupie. She was nineteen, red-headed, and worth one million dollars – *dead*! For Vickie was the key prosecution witness in a politically important trial and someone, somewhere was willing to stake a fortune to prevent her testifying. CURE had orders to keep her alive . . . not an easy mission – even for Remo Williams. And in the screaming chaos of the world's biggest rock festival ever, THE DESTROYER goes into action against the most expert assassins of the underworld. . . .

0 552 10017 X – 40p

THE DESTROYER: KILL OR CURE by RICHARD SAPIR and WARREN MURPHY

A man had been found with an ice-pick in his brain; the state of Florida was in an uproar; and CURE itself was in danger of being destroyed. A stupid and dangerous security leak meant an unwelcome scandal in the highest government offices and threatened the very lives of everyone even remotely connected with CURE. Remo Williams had just one week to perform his own particular brand of miracle – one week before CURE and all its operatives would be quietly and permanently erased. . . .

0 552 10018 8 – 40p

THE EXECUTIONER: PANIC IN PHILLY by DON PENDLETON

When the Executioner came to Philly – the city of brotherly love – it was with all the odds stacked against him. The ageing Don Stephano was importing hoods from the old country. These guys would ensure powerful support for his son who was to succeed him as boss of the Philadelphia Cosa Nostra. Don Stephano thought he was ready for Bolan . . . so did the cops who were swarming all over the town. But then the Executioner hit the scene and everyone had to start changing their minds. . . .

0 552 09814 0 – 40p

THE EXECUTIONER: MIAMI MASSACRE by DON PENDLETON

Mack Bolan is informed that Mafia overlords are meeting in Florida to make arrangements to wipe him out – permanently! He penetrates their inner council, only to encounter the guns of the dreaded Talifero brothers. They are skilled enforcers whose cold-blooded modus operandi makes them powerful foes to be feared and respected – even by The Executioner!

But when Bolan the death machine moves into action, striking back with devastating force and cunning at the very nerve centre of the Mafia – the Capos themselves – it's the enforcers' blood that flows. . . .

0 552 09204 5 – 40p

THE DESTROYER: JUDGEMENT DAY by RICHARD SAPIR and WARREN MURPHY

A 'protected' house is a relatively new development in the heroin trade. Instead of sending pushers out into the streets, where they can be ripped off by junkies, junkies go to these houses to get a fix on the premises. Protected houses are well supplied with weapons and have many fine locks, thick doors, and barred windows. The one in Detroit was no exception.
For the fifty-five kilo heroin consignment, special precautions were taken. Extra men with guns were placed inside the window openings. The front door was reinforced, the windows were nailed shut, the basement doors boarded.

It was a perfect defence. Against just about anything but a book of matches and a gallon of gasoline. As Remo Williams watched the front of the house flame up to become a funeral pyre for its inhabitants and an incinerator for the fifty-five kilos, he thought he heard the cab driver crying. . . .

0 552 10156 7 – 60p

THE DESTROYER: MURDER'S SHIELD by RICHARD SAPIR and WARREN MURPHY

Convicted and condemned to death for a crime he didn't commit, Remo Williams has been resurrected and re-programmed – not as a normal human being, but as a cold, calculating death machine . . . created to destroy in order to preserve . . . a lethal weapon that has no loyalties, and can only be used in extreme emergencies. . . .

They called themselves the Men of the Shield – they were a national organisation of policemen, formed to wipe out criminals the law could not reach. Forty of their number served as a killer squad, to mete out their own brand of justice. The death they dealt in was not pretty. Remo Williams now faced his toughest assignment – to eliminate this group before all hell let loose throughout the U.S.A.

0 552 09801 9 – 40p

A SELECTED LIST OF CRIME STORIES
FOR YOUR READING PLEASURE

All these books are available at your bookshop or newsagent; or can be ordered direct from the publisher. Just tick the titles you want and fill in the form below.

CORGI BOOKS, Cash Sales Department, P.O. Box 11, Falmouth, Cornwall.

Please send cheque or postal order, no currency.

U.K. send 19p for first book plus 9p per copy for each additional book ordered to a maximum charge of 73p to cover the cost of postage and packing.

B.F.P.O. and Eire allow 19p for first book plus 9p per copy for the next 6 books, there after 3p per book.

Overseas Customers. Please allow 20p for the first book and 10p per copy for each additional book.

NAME (block letters) ....

ADDRESS ....

(NOVEMBER 76) ....

While every effort is made to keep prices low, it is sometimes necessary to increase prices at short notice. Corgi Books reserve the right to show new retail prices on covers which may differ from those previously advertised in the text or elsewhere.